ANGEL RANGE

Books by John Reese

SURE SHOT SHAPIRO

THE LOOTERS

SUNBLIND RANGE

PITY US ALL

SINGALEE

HORSES, HONOR AND WOMEN

JESUS ON HORSEBACK: THE MOONEY COUNTY SAGA
ANGEL RANGE
THE BLOWHOLERS
THE LAND BARON

THE BIG HITCH

SPRINGFIELD .45-70

WEAPON HEAVY

THEY DON'T SHOOT COWARDS

JOHN REESE

ANGEL RANGE

ANGEL RANGE *first appeared as part
of the trilogy* JESUS ON HORSEBACK:
The Mooney County Saga

*Regards to Terry Orvis,
Sincerely
John Reese
Santa Maria
Jan. 1980*

DOUBLEDAY & COMPANY, INC.
GARDEN CITY, NEW YORK
1973

All of the characters in this book are purely fictional, and any resemblance to actual persons, living or dead, is coincidental.

ISBN: 0-385-03426-1
Library of Congress Catalog Card Number 79–181792
Copyright © 1971 by John Reese
All Rights Reserved
Printed in the United States of America

For Charles D. and Florence Reese

ANGEL RANGE

1

There was this outfit that sometimes worked as many as forty men, the Flying V, north of the Platte, and up toward Nebraska and also Wyoming, but still in Colorado and no nesters yet. That was where Rolf Ledger was heading on his sorry old bay horse. It was about where he wanted to locate for a while, and an outfit that worked a big crew was prob'ly going to be more liable than most to hire a man whose last job had been breaking rocks in the Kansas penitentiary.

Rolf had cinched his belt up to the last hole, and he was still gant and hungry, and had come down to where he was ready to coax for a job if he had to. You get as hungry as he was and you start peeling down your pride, and sometimes you find it turns out to be more shucks than nubbin.

Rolf had rode all the way up from Denver, and was still boiling. What happened, he hired out to a saloon to help build on a room, a dollar and a half a day and a place to sleep, only this fella he was working for, some way he figgered out that Rolf was an ex-convict. So after five days, he throwed him five two-bit pieces and told him to get out of Denver or he'd have him throwed in jail, and he could do it too.

So here Rolf was, looking for the Flying V, when he looked back and seen these people coming after him. He counted eight, and they sure wasn't saving their horses. So he just said to himself, Well if it's another dad-blamed posse, why to heck with them! Dad-blamed if I ain't getting fed up with the law.

A couple of them split off and headed west, like in case Rolf took a notion to hit for the brush. He knowed then that it was a posse sure enough, and it made him so sick of the whole mess of life that he started to shake, being so hungry anyway. For two cents he would of shot it out, only he knowed that shooting it out is a losing proposition, especially on a no-account horse like his'n, with its spring just about run down. So he just clumb out of the saddle to rest the horse, and slipped its bit to let it feed a little, and waited.

This fella on the big bay, he was the sheriff. They always have to have a big showy horse after they been in there a few years, and this sheriff had been in since Hector was the pup as the saying is, a real big man with quite a bit of fat, and long gray hair that he kept combed in a kind of a sweat-horse roach, and a big nose like a doorknob, and a big loud voice that could rattle your windows. But still a mighty good old man, with two pearl-handled .45 pistols, and a .30-30 carbine in a boot on his saddle, and you just knowed they wasn't for show.

He pulled up and waved his ham of a hand to stop his posse, and them two fellas that had took the west trail to cut Rolf off, they rode up too, and there Rolf was, surrounded by a sheriff and seven saddle-sore citizens that looked mighty upset at life.

The sheriff said, "Hello there, mister, is that gun loaded, I suppose?"

Rolf nodded and said, "Yes sir, Sheriff, it sure is. I always found there's nothing unhandier than an unloaded gun, when you have to shoot at something."

"Well, mister, then I want you to put both of your hands up nice and slow," the sheriff said, "and we'll just relieve you of that there loaded gun."

Rolf spread his hands out, but he didn't raise them. He said, "Sheriff, my horse hasn't got a bit in his mouth, and I might lose him if I let go."

The sheriff looked that old horse over and then said, "I reckon we could make do to run him down. Thad, take the gentleman's weapon, if you please."

Rolf let go the reins and lifted his hands, and his horse just leaned on three legs and went to sleep, purely shaming him. One of the posse got down to take Rolf's gun. He was a young fella about Rolf's age, about twenty-three, with a kind of an ignorant farmer expression, and a kind of a sheepish grin. Rolf said to him, "That's the wrong way to go at this, pardner, getting between me and your posse. If I was a mind to, I could have my gun out and use you for cover against the rest of them, only I ain't of a mind to."

The sheriff said, "Thad, you haven't got a Goddamn lick of sense," but Rolf let this kid Thad take his gun, and then the sheriff nodded for him to put his hands down if he wanted, and Rolf did.

"What's your name?" the sheriff said.

"Rolf Ledger," Rolf said. The sheriff told him how do you spell it; so he done that.

"Where'd you come from?"

"Denver last."

"Where'd you spend last night?"

"Camped on some dad-blamed creek out there amongst a bunch of dad-blamed Kincaiders and their old sore-backed horses. You could hear chickens crowing and shotes squealing until it would make you sick what's happening to the range, if you rode for a living."

"We don't speak against the homestead class in this county. We don't celebrate their coming, but so long as they keep their place, they don't have no trouble. Just remember that. What did you eat last night for supper?"

"A spring cottontail."

"Sure it wasn't somebody's chicken?"

Rolf was getting tired of all this, so he said, "It had four legs and long ears, and I never seen a chicken like that in all my born days, Sheriff. I up and shot it. It looked wild to me. It didn't have no brand on it, and I didn't have no idee it belonged to anybody."

"One little old cottontail size of a barn rat," the sheriff said. "You must not of had much appetite."

"I had plenty of appetite, but that's as close as I could get with a .45, one dad-blamed rabbit. I'm a pretty fair shot, Sheriff, but I ain't one of them gunnies you hear about that can pump three shots out and bring down three frisky young cottontails in the dusk. I often wished I was, but I ain't."

"All that is just talk," the sheriff said. "They ain't nobody can shoot that good. Thad, let's look in his bedroll. I don't see no rifle or other gun there, but let's look."

This young deputy kind of excused himself to Rolf, and untied his blanket from behind the saddle. He said, "A pair of brown wool pants and a razor strop and a wrapped-up razor in a pair of socks, is all. You want I should look in his saddlebags too?"

The sheriff said he might as well, so this Thad done it, and he said, "I'm a ringtailed son of a bitch, Abe, but will you look at what this man reads to pass the time? The Holy Bible, the Holy Rosary, the Holy Scripture, and the Book of Common Prayer."

"Are you a preacher, Ledger?" the sheriff said. "You don't look like much of a preacher to me, with a forty-five on you, and no shave and all."

"No, I ain't a preacher," Rolf said. "You won't rest easy until you know, even if it is none of your dad-blamed business. I helped the chaplain in the Kansas penitentiary, and he give me them books. And to lope ahead and cut off your next question before it gets its tail up, I got pardoned."

The sheriff said, "It beats me, how every ex-convict I run into got pardoned. None of you was ever guilty and just done your time, no sir, there's a poor old mother had faith in you, and the jury that convicted you like to died of remorse, and they got up a petition, and the governor broke his ass to pardon you. I never knowed it to fail, Mr. Ledger."

Rolf said, "Sheriff, they got a saying in the pen, the easiest way to beat your time is to die young. Well, I had better luck. The guilty party, a fella by the name of Bobby Dale, made a deathbed confession. The dirty low wheat-farming Kincaiders on the jury wouldn't of raised a hand for me, but the chaplain was on my side, and he got the warden on my side. The luck of the draw, Sheriff. I made my hand with them two cards."

The sheriff asked him what he was in for, and Rolf said murder, and the sheriff said, "Well, all I can do is turn you loose. The party we're looking for rode a real good little brown or black mare, and you'd have six hundred dollars in gold on you if you was him, and there might be some buckshot in you because this man was fired at with a shotgun. Just to be sure, Mr. Ledger, I don't reckon you'll mind taking off your clothes."

It wasn't something Rolf would of done for pleasure, but he had learned in the pen that there was times a man had to be humble, so he took off every stitch, even his socks, and proved he didn't have no buckshot in him. So the sheriff told him to get dressed. Rolf asked him what this fella they was looking for had done.

"Murder and robbery, that's what," the sheriff said. He said the victim was Colonel Pegler T. Saymill, a bachelor who lived in this county seat of Mooney, Colorado, with an old-maid sister to take care of him. He was better than seventy-five at the time of death, but he dyed his hair and had false teeth and starved himself to keep a fine limber figure. A ladies' man to the last.

Colonel Pegler T. Saymill had a lot of money loaned out, and this was what he lived on, the payments and interest, and lived mighty well. One of his loans was to Calvin Venaman, owner of the Flying V that Rolf had heard of, and the day before this, Cal had come in and made a six-hundred-dollar payment. All in gold.

Well, this morning the sister of Colonel Pegler T. Saymill was out in her garden behind her orchard, hoeing her garden, because you could bet the colonel wasn't going to raise a hand there. She didn't see anything that happened, but she knowed the six hundred dollars was in the drawer of the parlor desk.

"It was somebody Peg knowed, you can bet," the sheriff said. "There wasn't no other reason to kill him, unless he knowed Peg could testify against him in court. Peg was just cold-bloodedly shot in the chest, at arm's length, after handing over the money. It just blowed the poor old man in two, like."

The sister didn't hear that shot, but next door there was a

Dutchman by the name of Frank Mueller ran the meat market, and he also had a young orchard. He was out there chasing somebody's milk cow out of it, and he heard this shot and knowed something was wrong. He knowed the colonel didn't have no gun, because he had liked to shot himself with the last one he owned, and the sister took it away from him and give it to an Indian.

Frank run into the house and got the only weapon he had, an old Ithaca twelve. He never did get a good look at the fella, but he yelled to ask what the shooting was about, and he seen somebody leading a horse out behind the trees and vines, so he just let go with the shotgun. The robber let go with two from his pistol through the trees, and Frank run into the house, in the interests of staying alive.

"Nobody else seen him," the sheriff said, "but I can testify it was a hell of a horse he rode, because it took some fences your ordinary cayuse wouldn't tackle getting out of there. All we know about it is what Frank said, through the trees it was either brown or black. We run out of tracks soon as he hit the prairie. We seen where you had your bonfire last night, and skinned and cooked your rabbit about four miles from town."

"I don't know this country and I never been in Mooney," Rolf said, "and I'm riding the wrong horse, and let me tell you if I ever commit a murder and rob anybody of six hundred dollars, I ain't going to stop a few miles out to build a fire and cook a cottontail. I'm going to make tracks. Nothing personal meant, Sheriff, but it seems to me I've seen better police work done in my time."

"Don't get smart," the sheriff said. "I don't apologize a bit for stopping you. I run this county, and I run it my way, and any time there's a murder in it, a stranger has got to explain himself, especially if he turns out to be an ex-convict. Nothing personal meant on my part either, but you're a real ragged-ass specimen to be criticizing the law."

"Well, that's the way I am," Rolf said. "I won't fight, and I'm on the side of the law generally, but any time I feel like speaking out, I'm going to speak out."

Rolf was about five-nine high, weighing no more than one hundred and thirty-eight, and limber as a snake from being on short rations so long. He had on the blue denim pants he had wore out of the pen, and a blue hickory shirt, and a brown Texas hat he had bought in a second-hand store for six bits. He knowed he didn't cut much of a figger, and was prob'ly tetchy about it.

"You go right ahead and speak out, and if your ass lands in jail, you bet your last cent I'll have a case against you," this sheriff said. "Let's see them books of yours."

He clumb down off'n his horse, and Thad handed him the books, and he looked them over and said, "I be damned! What the hell's the difference between a Holy Bible and a Holy Scriptures, Mr. Ledger?"

"It's the Jewish Bible, is all," Rolf said.

"Is that a fact! How come they got a different Bible than every other person on earth?"

"It's a different religion."

"Is that a fact! You read a lot about the Jews in our Bible, in fact that's just about all there is in it. How does it happen to be a different religion?"

"It's too long to explain here."

"Is that a fact!" the sheriff said. "My mother claimed her mother was a Jew, but my daddy said no, she was a Spaniard. I reckon he was right. I remember the old lady myself, and she could talk Spanish. I learned my first Spanish from Grandma Rowan. Her maiden name was Lanfranco. But I remember her as Grandma Rowan."

Rolf said, "She could of been both. The chaplain said there was a strain of Jew, the Sephardic strain, that is both Jewish and Spanish."

"Is that a fact! So you think the old lady, my grandmother, could of been one of them?"

"She could, but what difference does it make?"

The sheriff said, "Mr. Ledger, it's an election year this year, and I've had my problems, one of them being this Goddamn robbery and murder of Colonel Saymill. You either run on your record of law enforcement, or you run on character and things like that. I could be the only law enforcement officer in Colorado that's part Spanish Jew. Them things take the fancy of a voter. What is this Book of Common Prayer?"

Rolf explained that it was what the Episcopalians used, and it went all the way back to Henry the Eight, and even farther.

The sheriff said, "Is that a fact! How about the Rosary, though? You can't fool me, that's Catholic, and I know enough about that sect to know that a person like you can't do nobody any good with it. You have got to be a priest in good standing, not just some old ragged-ass cowboy that happens to have the right books along."

Rolf said, "That ain't necessarily so. We had mostly Methodists and Babtists and so on in the pen, and there wasn't business enough to keep a priest on steady. One used to come around once a month to take confessions, but in the case of a dying man, anybody that was babtized a Christian could take the last confession and grant extreme unction, and it's legal."

"Now, Mr. Ledger, I just plain don't believe that!" the sheriff said. "Why, they won't even let their girls marry out of the sect! How could you do that?"

"I done it three times, as a favor to the chaplain when he wasn't around, and we had prisoners up and die on us without warning."

The sheriff scratched his jaw and said, "If we had made a mistake and strung you up, I reckon you'd of met your Maker with just about every endorsement there is. How come you to take on them chores in prison?"

"The chaplain made me his assistant."

"You ever preach a sermon?"

"No, I never was ordained. I only—"

"What's ordained?"

"Swore in as a preacher. When the chaplain was out on circuit on Sunday, I held services as a favor to him, that's all. He was always working on me to be a dad-blamed preacher, but helping him out was as fur as I was ready to go, and I done that only because time hangs so heavy on your hands in prison, and besides it got me out of my cell even more than a trusty."

"By God, if this ain't a piece of luck!" the sheriff said. "Brother Richardson, the Methodist preacher in Mooney, moved out on us several months ago. Blessed Sacrament is only a mission, and Father Lavrens only hits it to count his flock every week or so, and there wouldn't be no use asking him to bury Peg Saymill because Peg professed atheism. But somebody's got to do it, and you look like the right man to me."

"I ain't," Rolf said, "and anyway if he was an atheist, what difference does it make how he's buried?"

"It makes a difference to his sister, and anybody that had as much money as Colonel Pegler T. Saymill, it's pure blasphemy to spade him under without the proper orgies. You come on back and bury him, and I'll bet Liz Saymill will part with a five-dollar bill. No, I won't take no for an answer, Mr. Ledger, or I might say Reverend. A town without a church is a discredit, and a church without a preacher is no church at all, and it's an election year. Mount up, boy, and let's get going!"

"No thank you," Rolf said. "I only want to get to the Flying V, and get me a job if I can."

This here young deputy, Thad, said, "You can't. He'll just run you off the place with a prison record, the old son of a bitch."

"And Thad knows," the sheriff said, "because Cal has got two daughters, and Thad is sweet on one of them. If a deputy sheriff ain't fit for one of them, he sure won't take no chance on an ex-convict!"

"I was pardoned, I told you," Rolf said.

"Cal won't stand on technicalities. No sir, you come back and conduct a decent Christian funeral over this old money-grubbing son of a bitch, and then let's see what we can work out for you. You're at a crossroads in life, as the fella says, and I like to help a young man to go straight when I can," the sheriff said.

Rolf would of argued, only his knees kind of give way from pure starvation, and he had to own up how long since he had et a square meal. Them bloodthirsty public citizens on the posse had rode out with nothing to eat in their saddlebags. They had fed at a couple of ranches as they loped around looking for tracks, but all they had on them was chewing tobacco.

And as Rolf told them, he had give up chewing and smoking, as well as cursing, fighting, drinking, and other forms of public misbehavior, to hang onto his job as assistant to the chaplain. He was at their mercy, you might say. On the way back to town, they spotted some wild strawberries that had just come in, it being spring, and they all got down to help him pick, and it helped. No man can pick enough wild strawberries to fill him up, but with eight helpers it's a different proposition.

2

They had to take it slow on the way back to Mooney, on account of Rolf's sorry old horse, and the sheriff nagged at him until he got what you might call the story of his life. Rolf Ledger had made most of his own troubles, and he owned up to it. He said he knowed he was unjustly convicted and sentenced, but there wasn't no use pining, he had to make the best of it, even if there ain't much that's best in life for murder.

Rolf come from a respectable family in Smith County, only him and an older brother and sister, and his mother and father. Rolf's father was a wheat buyer. Everybody was wheat-crazy then. It was just wheat, wheat, wheat, and many a good piece of prairie was plowed up to make middling-bad wheat land.

Rolf's mother was a good sensible Swede woman, and it was her that had give him the name of Rolf, and her that run the store with the help of Rolf's brother Eddie, and kept food on the table when wheat prices went the wrong way. Them Swedes is good steady people when they're not drinking, and her family never touched it.

Eddie was good in the store, and the sister, Katie, married a good steady man, a Rock Island telegraph operator, but all Rolf ever wanted to be was a trapper or a cowboy or a train robber. He got in with the Cohelan gang before he was seventeen, while Denny Cohelan was still alive, before he got shot by a mere boy of fifteen for getting gay with his sister. In fact Rolf was at that same dance, and would be the first to tell you that Denny Cohelan stood pat when he should of drawed cards.

Rolf went up to the Black Hills with Holbrook Cohelan the next summer. Nobody around Smith County knowed what happened there, but Rolf came back that fall in a mighty ructious frame of mind, and Holbrook come back a few weeks later looking peaked from a bullet in his belly that was still healing. The gossip was that Rolf had lost all respect for Holbrook Cohelan, because they sure wasn't friends no more, and pretty soon Holbrook left town.

If Rolf earned twenty honest dollars that year, it was by mighty secret labor. Mostly he was in and out of his daddy's house, he'd leave when the old man rode him too hard about being worthless, and come back when he got lonesome or hungry, like with most kids.

The last time he come back, it was just in time to get arrested for robbery and murder of the Missouri Pacific agent in Coffeyville that paid only $76.50. Rolf was *out* of Smith Center when it happened, that was sure, and he rode back *in* with Stephen A. Douglas Latimer, and both Latimer and Holbrook Cohelan had been seen in Coffeyville at the time of the murder, and Cohelan couldn't be found nowhere afterward.

Latimer chose to shoot it out in Smith County, and was killed dead without saying a word either way about the robbery, or about anything else. Nobody knowed where Holbrook Cohelan had went to, and in fact it was the last time he was

ever heard of in connection with being the head of a gang of
robbers, or of anything. It was poor shakes as a robbery, and
people reckoned he had give up on robbery as a life's work.

The third member of the gang was supposed to be Rolf. Nobody had got a real good look at him, but people was getting
tired of his quarrelsomeness and general worthless disposition
anyway, and there wasn't no tears shed outside of his family
when he was found guilty by a jury. They wasn't out no more
than fifteen minutes, just long enough to make sure they got
fed by the county.

"You got anything to say before I pass sentence?" the judge
asked Rolf.

"I don't know what good it would do," Rolf said.

"Prob'ly none," the judge said, "but that ain't the question,
you got the right to speak up now or forever hold your peace.
That's the law as I interpret it."

"Well then, all I can say is I didn't have nothing to do with
that Goddamn ignorant robbery. The jury acts like they know
a lot more of the facts than the witnesses that couldn't say they
recognized me. You just look at them shifty sons of bitches,
Judge, there ain't none of them man enough to look me in the
eye. They know in their hearts they condemned an innocent
man, if they had hearts."

"Mind your language in court," the judge said. "Is that all
you have to say?"

"There's more, but what good would it do?" Rolf said.

"Don't you even want to warn the jury that when you get
out, you'll come back and hunt them down and kill them if it's
your last act on earth?" the judge said.

"That would be the most useless thing I could say or do,
Judge," Rolf said. "Look at them! They're just a bunch of ignorant wheat farmers; how can you expect better of such miserable bastards? I reckon I brung this on myself by not trying to
scratch me a living on a homestead myself, but I ain't sorry. If
I was as ignorant as them, they'd take pity on me and say turn
that poor boy loose, life is hard enough on him. But I tried to
have some fun out of life. The wrong kind of fun you'll say, but

what the hell is the right kind in this Godforsaken country, since they plowed up the grass to raise wheat and nobody can afford to hire a good cowhand?"

The judge let him get it out of his system, and he told him he had saved himself a good hanging by not harboring a spirit of vengeance against the jury, and then he sentenced him to life in prison. He said it was partly because of Rolf's attitude and partly because there wasn't no real good identification of him, only circumstantial evidence, and he didn't like to hang a man on that.

"I don't know what's to be thankful for, setting on my rump in prison the rest of my life," Rolf said. "You mean well, Judge, but Goddamn it, you don't have to do the time there, and I do."

"Well, that's true, and I know what you mean about this once being a good cow country, and I take judicial notice of it," the judge said. "I don't know if the people changed the country, or the country changed the people, or what. But I'm stirrup to stirrup with you on wheat, and another thing I detest is mules."

"You're right there, all right," Rolf said. "Mules are all right in the Army, but nowhere else."

"Right as rain! I don't mind a man raising mules to sell to the Army. But when I see these poor misguided people riding a harrow or a gang plow behind four mules, without a brood mare on the place, I wonder what this country is coming to. Where are their draft animals coming from next time? Buy them, that's all they can do!" the judge said.

"That's sure the truth! But people can only see the almighty dollar. A mule will turn out more work on less feed, yes, and that's as far as fools like these fools on the jury can think."

The judge said, "Well, look on yourself, young man, as a mule for the future, and go up there to the pen and resolve to be a good mule. You sure ain't going to procreate in no prison, and you are going to work, and if you have to be a mule, I say be a good one!"

"Well, I'll tell you how I feel about that point of view," Rolf

said. "HEEEEE—HAW!" He just let out the most raucous and
lifelike bray that prob'ly was ever heard in a United States
courtroom. And that ended the trial. Well Rolf went to the
prison, and got his head shaved, and was issued a shirt and
pants and shoes but no underwear or socks, and he worked on
the rock pile long enough to have a favorite sledge hammer.
There wasn't really any difference, one sledge hammer was
about like another sledge hammer, but convicts would stake
out a claim on one, and know it by its feel, and you could get
your head caved in for taking some other convict's sledge
hammer.

Then this chaplain by the name of James Elroy, a Babtist
by conviction but not too hardshell to sympathize with a Presbyterian or a Catholic or a Socialist, especially if he had to
hang, came around and asked Rolf if there was anything he
could do for Rolf. Rolf said he reckoned not, everything was
going pretty smooth; making little ones out of big ones wasn't
his idea of sheer fun, but he reckoned he had got himself into
it even if he was innocent, by his general worthlessness. They
got to be friends, and this chaplain said he thought he could
get Rolf out of his cell and off'n the rock pile if he would go for
being his assistant.

Rolf felt pretty sheepish about it at first, but he just dared
anybody to make any remarks. He got the swing of it pretty
fast, and learned to rattle off a prayer as easy as swatting flies
on a cold day when they're not very spry, and mostly the job
was praying with some fool that had come to his regrets too
late, in prison. He never figured he'd have to take any Catholic's last confession, and forgive him his sins, or hold a funeral
for somebody that jumped off and landed on his head because
he couldn't stand prison no longer.

But when them jobs was dealt him, he made the best showing he could, and the other convicts got to where they stopped
cursing and talking dirty around him, and in fact avoided him
all they could except when they was in trouble. It got pretty
lonesome, but it was still better than setting in his cell or breaking rocks.

Then this fellow Bobby Dale, who had busted out of the Arkansas pen where he was doing life for robbing an old woman and accidentally smothering her to death, he got shot in a stick-up. He kept a pillow on the woman's face to shut up her screaming, and he accidentally kept it there too long, and then after he got out and got shot, he admitted it was him and not Rolf that had been in on the Missouri Pacific robbery with Holbrook Cohelan and Stephen A. Douglas Latimer.

He told a few things about that murder that nobody could of knowed unless they was there, so it couldn't be a mistake, he done it and not Rolf. It took almost a year to ding the governor into listening, the main trouble being none of them jurymen felt like signing any petitions, not after the way Rolf had talked about them and wheat farmers in general at the trial. But finally the governor got tired of being dinged about it, so he signed a pardon and said good riddance, this fellow was more trouble in prison than he ever could be out of it.

Rolf told the sheriff about it as they ambled back to town, and it was actually a relief to him to have somebody to talk to about it, although he would ruther of been up there at the Flying V, with his feet under a good table, and a good job waiting for him as soon as he got through feeding himself. But this sheriff was something like that chaplain, he drawed a man out in spite of his best intentions, and any time you pull a gun on an ex-convict and then let him have it back and call him "mister," you've at least got him wondering.

This sheriff was Abe Whipple, a man who had been in the law-enforcement business since he helped lynch a claim jumper in the silver country at age seventeen. He was a big huge ignorant loudmouthed man, but he had proved time and again that his intentions was good, and nobody ever doubted he had the guts to go with the job.

He said, "Mr. Ledger, I always said we had the most ignorant people in the world in Mooney County, but from what you tell me, Smith County, Kansas, is afflicted with some dandies there too."

"You're right loose with your talk, ain't you, about people you have to ask to vote for you," Rolf said.

Abe said, "Oh hell, I don't ask them, I tell them. I run this county the way it should be run. What people want is peace and order, and the less cheating by merchants and saloon-keepers, the better, and anybody can pack a gun but they better not pull it in town. I don't bother to go down to the courthouse at all, unless I've got somebody in jail there. I run my job from my house, and if them county officials want to see me, they can come there. Of course you got to amuse people too, that's true. But wait till they hear I'm part Spanish Jew! That'll just charm the hell out of them. People like to think they're different from other counties, you see."

Rolf admitted that was true, even in prison. The sheriff asked how could that be, and Rolf told him. He said:

"I went into that prison real sore, I can sure tell you that, but them old hands there, they'll tell you that pining and re-gretting just makes it worse. Then this chaplain got me to stop cursing and chewing tobacco and losing my temper. Them's the only bad habits you can enjoy in prison, and it gives you plenty to do to break them.

"There's another thing you can do, fight. You ain't supposed to fight, but if there's no other way to settle it, you go to the captain and tell him, and he sets up a fight so nobody gets killed. I had some fights that done me a lot of good, even them I lost, before I had to swear off them too.

"How this happened, I was out on the rock pile, and the fella chained to me asked me for a chew, and I told him I was completely broke of the habit, and of cursing and fighting too. He said he never in all his life heard the like, and this was his third prison, counting one in England. He talked it around, and pretty soon about half of the convicts was swearing off cursing and chewing and fighting, just to be different.

"Well then one Sunday, the captain that run the graft where you bought thread and tobacco and a sheet of paper to write home twice a year, he called a meeting before chapel. He said, 'It looks like we got a purity movement going here, nobody is chewing any more. What do you pure sons of bitches think I'm going to do with a whole case of chewing tobacco? This foolishness has got to stop. When you line up for supper, show a plug of chewing or you lose five marks.'

"They paid you a dime a day for breaking rocks, but they charged you a penny to rent your sledge hammer, and a penny insurance so you could go to the infirmary if you broke a bone or something, and a penny for the cooks to take the pebbles out of the beans and the rat turds out of the rice, and a penny for I forget what. So all you really got was six cents, and every time they punished you by taking away five marks, there went another penny.

"That's how it was done. The captain didn't hardly make anything on the smoking tobacco. The profit was all in the plug. A lot of them convicts was just spirited enough to swear off for life when the captain said that, and I knowed I was going to have everybody in trouble.

"So I stood up and excused myself, and I told the captain I had started it for the chaplain, and my advice was just to let it run its course. And he said, 'Your advice, well I like that, I'll tell you what my advice to you is, you come out of chapel with a plug of tobacco in your hand or you go to the Hole.' I told him I had swore off due to religion, and it was against the law to make a man do what was against his religion. They couldn't make a Catholic eat the side pork in his beans on a Friday, or a Jew eat it any time, not that we ever had any problem with being fed too much meat.

"Then we had to go to chapel, and things quietened down more than somewhat, but them convicts just went plumb out of their heads afterward. I heard that when they went to mess for supper, they wouldn't show a plug of tobacco, and they banged their tin plates around and hollered and dared the screws to shoot, and they got away with it. Of course they wanted to be ornery, too, but at the start, swearing off was only being different, like you said."

Abe said, "Do tell! You say you *heard* this was what went on, where was you all this time?"

"In the Hole, solitary confinement. An old cistern with eight inches of stinking water in it, and dead rats floating in it, and nothing to set on," Rolf said.

"I couldn't stand that very long, Mr. Ledger, or I might say Reverend Ledger," Abe said.

Rolf said, "Don't call me that! I wouldn't take it from them fellas in prison, and I don't have to take it from you. Sheriff, you can stand anything when the time comes you have to. You get a man mad enough, and he has already swore off cursing and fighting and losing his temper, what has he got left but self-control? You wouldn't of knowed me, if you had knowed me before I went to prison. If I let myself go, thinking about that jury, I could of went crazy there in the Hole. So as fur as I would carry it was to wish I had some of them wheat farmers in there with me when they was worrying about a dry spell.

"Couple of times a day, the captain would lift the lid off and holler down and asked if I wanted a chew. I'd be setting there in the water, leaning back with my arms folded, with the water running down my back from that clammy old brick wall. And I'd say, 'Why God bless you for thinking of me, Captain, no I don't chew, but go in peace and remember the Commandment, Honor thy father and thy mother. That is, if you have any idee who your father was!' I still had this bitterness in me, you see."

"More bitterness than sense," Abe said. "You's in no shape to reflect on his mother's chastity, setting there in eight inches of water."

"Well, that's what too much self-control can do to you. I was in there five days and nights, and how I got out was that the chaplain come back from riding circuit, and he'd had a good trip, several weddings and funerals, and quite a few sinners had come to repentance. So he asked about me, and they told him I was in the Hole, where of course he couldn't see me. But by then they had themselves another problem in that prison, and they thought maybe he could help them with it.

"This whole prison had got religion or something, and they wasn't satisfied with swearing off chewing, no sir, they wouldn't even *eat* until their assistant chaplain was let out of the Hole. They'd go out there and just keel over by the dozen on the rock pile, from hunger, and every time one did, everybody else would start screaming. The screws didn't care to risk shooting, because you take a bunch of men who simply don't care, numbers count."

Abe said, "Yes, you'll drop a few, but then the others are on you with their bare hands."

"Yes. Anyway they let him fish me out and dry me off, and bring me a cup of water and some cold noodles. He said frankly he never heard of anybody carrying his faith to extremes the way I had, since they quit burning heretics. A heretic is somebody that don't agree with you," Rolf said.

"He said, 'Ledger, I personally think you're more vain than penitent, but you have a start toward being a real Christian. What have you got to lose by going the rest of the way? Do you want these men to die of starvation, or go crazy and be shot by the guards? Don't tell me this is a matter of principle! Tell me this, have you ever been babtized?'

"I said no, unless you could count setting in that Hole. He said that was a form of babtism after all, and why not go for the pure-D form, and own up to my stubborn vanity, and then help get them idiots back to the mess hall. He said, 'What do you want, their deaths and your distinction, or peace of mind?' I said all I wanted was to be let alone and for them fellas to have a square meal.

"He said, 'I can get them the square meal if you can get them to eat it. But being let alone, that's out of my power. We have to rub elbows with our brothers in Christ, as enemies or as real brothers. You can't run from it. All your life you been trying to and look where it landed you! Ledger, the Lord is holding out His hand to you, and you're too cowardly to take it.'

"I said look what I'd been through and hadn't caved in, how could he call me a coward? He said, 'Ledger, a martyr to faith

is a hero, but a martyr to his own vanity is a wicked fool.' I
tried to hold out, Sheriff, but them noodles was beginning to
melt down in me, and I just felt so good I had a moment of
weakness, and I said all right.

"He hollered for a trusty to bring a tin cup of water, and
he made me kneel down there sopping wet and all wrinkled
up from being so long in the water, and he babtized me and
made me a Christian. Then he got me some more noodles.

"I told him I didn't feel any different, and I still couldn't
swaller everything I read in the Bible, and if the Bible was
one hundred percent the word of God, then all I could say
was that God had His own problems. He said a little doubt
never hurt anybody, just make sure I didn't let it become a
vice like I did self-control, you can run anything into the
ground.

"So that's how it is, Sheriff. I'll bury your dead atheist, do
the best job I can on him, but I don't think it's going to do a bit
of good. What goes in a prison is one thing. The Lord has
mighty slim pickings there anyway, but I can't see Him taking
my word for anything on the outside."

Sheriff Abe Whipple thought this over a long time while
they jogged along, and then he said, "Well, I'm afraid I have
to differ with you. I reckon your writ runs outside as well as in.
Let's see what kind of a sermon you preach."

"I ain't going to preach a sermon. I'll lead in prayer and
recite the eulogy, if somebody will give me a few tips to go
on, and I don't reckon I'll have any trouble there. In prison,
it's hard to eulogize anybody, all you can say generally is he
took his weekly bath and never let himself stink, and would
share his tobacco or his stub pencil with you. Things like that."

The sheriff said, "You know what I've got in mind, Mr.
Ledger. Here's a church that is short a preacher, and here's a
preacher that is short a job. No, it won't do you no good to
holler at me! Let's see how things work out. If you suit the
church board, and we can find some way for you to support
yourself, it could solve a lot of problems, one of them being an
empty, idle church in an election year. And I might say here
and now, young man, I ain't asking you, I'm telling you!"

3

Rolf took a shine to Mooney, Colorado, the minute he seen it. There wasn't no mountains there, but it stood high enough to be seen for some distance off, and was old enough for the trees the old settlers had planted to of growed up pretty good. It wasn't no small town either, claiming 414 people according to the best guesses. It got started as a halfway station during the Indian troubles, or the cavalry troubles as some people said, the cavalry being as much of a nuisance as the Indians at times. It had outgrowed its old wild beginnings, except for one thing.

This was a part of town most people ignored, or if they had to mention it, they only said "across the crick." Mooney laid between two lines of the Burlington, also called the C.B.&Q., or often just the Q, with no rail service in town, but not far from Sterling or Fort Morgan, if you could spare a day for the trip.

If you didn't have a whole day, you made do with what was in Mooney or across the crick. You might as well come right out and say this was the red-light zone, with five or six hotels, and a couple of saloons with a game usually going in them, and if you had the money to afford it, Huey Haffener's Jackrabbit Club, where they offered the most refined and expensive worldly pleasures. They had a store or two, and a livery barn strictly for their own people, and Dr. Sidney Nobile's office, a better doctor in many diseases than the ones in Fort Morgan or Sterling, especially for female complaints.

The people that lived there, and the cowboys and freighters

that spent their money there, called it Lickety Split, but in Mooney they only said "across the crick." It laid kind of low, and about every other spring it got flooded when the spring backed up, and they always had mosquitoes. There used to be a saying that a man never noticed the mosquitoes until he was *leaving* Lickety Split, but this is just a point of human nature and has nothing to do with Rolf Ledger.

It was onto dark by the time they got to town. Abe took Rolf to his house, and had his woman feed him, and give him a room where he could put on his brown wool pants and prepare himself spiritually for his ordeal. Mrs. Whipple was the former Edna McHenry when she married the sheriff, only he wasn't sheriff then, just another cowboy with nothing to mark his future greatness except his nerve. She had a ham boiling with spring greens, and a dried-apple pie, and she was famous for her good, strong coffee with plenty of bite in it, and if Rolf needed any proof that he was in a nice homey town, this was it.

Edna took his gun and hung it in the closet, and then he shaved and put on his brown wool pants, and when she seen his shirt, she decided she had time to whip up a clean white one for him. She cut one out, and basted it to his fit, and got it all done except the buttonholes before it was time for him to go, so she pinned it on him with the buttons sewed on the outside. "There, nobody is going to notice the difference, Reverend," she said.

Abe was hustling around town, organizing the crowd. There was some doubt about using the church, since the deceased had been a devoutly outspoken nonbeliever, and had turned down many a chance to write off a four-hundred-dollar church mortgage that he held. But in an election year, Abe wasn't going to be denied. He got the church.

Mooney had an embalmer, a builder by trade, very good on ornamental doors and bay windows, and he made his own coffins. Liz Saymill, the bereaved sister, told him to shoot the stack and bill the estate. The embalmer, Bernard Petty by name, had a bolt of lavender satin he had been saving for years. Most men called Bernard are going to end up Bernie or Barney or Benny, but this one stood on ceremony for the dignity of the dead, and was always called Bernard.

He done a good job on the colonel, and he had him laying there on lavender satin, outlined by a ruffle he cut with his wife's pinking shears, and he really slathered on the witch hazel and bay rum, so there wasn't hardly any smell of the chemicals in the colonel. He delivered the body in its coffin, stained ebony, to the church without any extra charge, and put on his pearl-gray gloves and stood watch beside it, not moving at all, not so much as to wrinkle his face to scare off a fly now and then, or bending his eyes to see whose kids was peeking in the windows. He just stood there reverently.

Abe got back when Rolf was ready to push back his chair from the table. "You'll have a good crowd, Reverend," he said, "and I can remember that church being filled only twice. Once was a revival that seemed to catch on one real dry summer eight years ago, and once when a Texas cowboy tried to devil an Indian by the name of Excuse Me Bill. He picked on the wrong Indian. I had to put Excuse Me Bill in jail for a day or two, the town being full of cowboys. At the funeral, we had one side of the church full of cowboys and the other side full of Indians. Brother Richardson got gas on his stomach from nervousness, and belched two or three times during the service, but I had my men swore in and scattered through the audience. There wasn't no trouble and they had better than thirty dollars in the collection plate."

"Getting up in front of a bunch of convicts was one thing," Rolf said, "but getting up in front of a lot of strangers kind of spooks me."

"You'll do fine! You look real good in them brown wool pants," Abe said.

"Your wife ironed them for me with a wet rag. I never seen that before," Rolf said.

"The only way to iron wool is with a wet rag over it, didn't you know that?" Abe said.

"No, as I say, I never seen it before," Rolf said.

"That Kansas must be a backward state if they don't even know how to iron wool. Let's go, Reverend," Abe said.

The closer Rolf got to the church, the worse he felt, but he was in for it and he knowed it. And when he seen that crowd, he would ruther have died himself than Colonel Saymill.

Most people could of walked there, but at a funeral it's human nature to want to ride, and spare your frail flesh all you can. The First Methodist was a big brown wooden building on log sills with the bark still on them, and them windows was something to behold. The Q had wrecked a passenger train up north of Mooney once, and turned over some fine new coaches with colored ornamental glass over the windows, and the Methodists got there even before the wrecker.

"Son of a bitch, there's Huey Haffener with some of his Jackrabbit ladies," the sheriff said. "He's asking a lot of a bunch of Methodists. What do you think?"

"If they was friends of the departed, I don't see how you can bar them," Rolf said.

"Well, but this don't seem to be the time and place to call attention to that friendship. I'll interduce you to Huey. He can tell you all you need to know about Peg, the good and the bad," Abe said.

People was going into church with that grim look people wear to funerals, but the sheriff put his fingers in his mouth and ripped out a whistle, and then he took off his hat and waved it to Huey, and Huey and his three girls come down the sidewalk and met them behind a lilac bush. Abe interduced Huey and Rolf, and then Huey interduced Amy, Babe, and Cherry, which he called the A, B, and C of it.

Huey was a twitchy man, kept rubbing his nose with his fingers and pawing the dirt with his shoes, and tightening and loosening his stomach muscles. His eyes was what you might call snot-colored, with big flabby suitcases under them. He dyed his hair black and parted it in the middle, and some said wore a corset.

"I had great respect for Peg," Huey said. "I can remember a dozen times he handed out money to down-and-out men,

not your worthy cases, and he never expected to get any of
it back, or any credit in heaven. No, Peg had no interest in a
man until genteel society had give up on him."

"Our Lord was kind to the same kind of people, when He
walked the earth," Rolf said.

"I doubt for the same reasons," Huey said. "Peg just liked to
take a long-shot bet against the world. He paid cash for everything and you never seen him in liquor. I can't think of anything else you could use in a sermon."

"Likewise," said Babe, and Amy nodded, and Cherry said,
"Peg cursed freely, but he never talked dirty, and he respected
Albert Sidney Johnston as the best general on either side in
the war except his own commander, a man by the name of Gib-
bons that was killed young. I can't think of anything else."

"Thanks for trying," Rolf said, and Huey and the girls went
back to the church and went in, and Rolf said, "My, they sure
are pretty girls."

"Just as nice as they are pretty," Abe said. "You don't see
Amy or Babe or Cherry getting drunk or diseased or tarred
and feathered. But somehow they're always glad to move over
and get a job with Bea Cunningham."

"Mr. Haffener must be quite a ladies' man," Rolf said.

"Well, he likes to be thought of as such, but I've knowed
him for fifteen years, and his girls all treat him more like a
sister. Let's talk to somebody else," Abe said.

They circulated around, and Rolf scraped up what he could
get for his eulogy, but the pickings was thin except that Peg
had wrote a beautiful hand and once had raised the best fighting chickens in Colorado, until his sister made him cut it out,
and things like that. And Rolf met Bernard Petty, and Bernard
said, "After the services, I would be glad to have you partake
of a little brandy in the settings of my funeral parlor, a toast to
the departed and a restorative to we who preside."

"I never touch the stuff," Rolf said, "but I appreciate the
thought, Mr. Petty."

He met Liz Saymill, a smart little old woman about as big
as twenty cents' worth of salt, with highborn manners that

went all the way back to her great-grandmother in Maine. She said, "So you're not ordained, well I'm sure a patient and tolerant God meant it to be. My brother was a quarrelsome rascal and a cynic, but he deserved better than to be shot down like a dog. I hope you won't have to compromise your own convictions to say a few words in behalf of one so hell-bent as Pegler."

"If he's hell-bent, I don't know it," Rolf said. "I doubt the Lord has even had time to find your brother's brand in the book let alone run him down the lower chute, ma'am. With all respect, I wouldn't bet a cent either one of us could predict how He's going to rule."

"That's a comfort," Liz said. "I took a quick judgment for granted, and that was wrong, wasn't it? I can shed a few tears now, and start worrying about my own soul, instead of pitying Pegler's in hell."

Rolf said he reckoned he had enough to slide through, and he wanted to get it over with before he lost his nerve, so they went in the side door, and the people still waiting out in front went in the front door. There was a little private room inside the side door, with a desk for the preacher, and a nail where he could hang his raincoat during services, although it wasn't safe overnight, and a locked cabinet for the communion wine. The sheriff took a book off'n the shelf and said, "This is the songbook they use. Pick yourself out what you want and I'll tell Mable, although I personally favor 'Lead, Kindly Light,' 'Up from the Dead,' and 'Till We Meet Again,' and the thing is, I know Mable can struggle them out of the organ. The others are a gamble."

Rolf said any tunes would do, just give him the numbers. So the sheriff wrote down the numbers, and went and told Mrs. Mable McMurdoch that these was the ones the reverend wanted, and she said, "Mighty curious that *he* favors the ones *you* favor, but I ain't going to question anybody's word at a time like this."

Rolf could hear the people stomping and kicking around to find seats, and when they quieted down, he knowed it was time for him to come out. And all of a sudden, it didn't bother him no more. It was like waiting to get on a horse you had bet you could ride that had throwed everybody else: you was nervous until it came your time, and then you just got on and rode him. Or got throwed, as the case may be, but it wasn't nerves that throwed you.

So he went out and found himself on the stage, on the lectern side. That's the left side from the preacher's standpoint in the Methodist faith, whatever it is elsewhere. He had both the Holy Bible and, on a hunch, the Book of Common Prayer. He went up and laid his two books on the lectern, and the only thing he really wished then was that he had a pair of glasses he could put on, and do it up right.

He took the sheriff's note out, and opened the book of hymns that was on the lectern. He looked around him, and he seen the coffin down there with this old white-headed dude in it, and every lamp in the church burning and one of them smoking, and the light twinkling off'n them red, blue, green, and orange glass panels from the Q passenger cars, and he just had the feeling he had catched his fourth jack and this pot was his'n.

He said, "The Lord is in His temple. Let us all rise and supplicate His mercy with a moment of silent prayer. When the organ begins, let us lift our hearts and our voices in 'Lead, Kindly Light,' which you will find on Page 147 of your hymnals. Let us bow our heads."

"Not for a minute, young man. You just hold it a minute, young man!" a woman said.

It was Mrs. Stella Landsdown, a former Babtist who wouldn't unite with any other church, who was dead against sin of all kinds, especially carnal sin, and she knowed more Deuteronomy on this subject than most preachers. She was standing up pretty close to the front, and pointing across the church at a woman who was just setting there with her hat on with a feather in it, in the same pew as Huey Haffener and his three Jackrabbit girls.

Rolf said, "What's the matter, ma'am, what ails you?" and

she said, "I suppose we have to tolerate Mr. Haffener, the Methodists are notoriously lax, but even they don't have to put up with the likes of Beatrice Cunningham. This is a house of worship and either she leaves or I do! I don't have to tell anybody why either, and I bet I take plenty with me, the cream of Christianity in this town too, and will you look at that silk dress. Silk! Out, I want her out of here!"

She was just screaming at the end. Rolf knowed that all he had to do was look to Abe, in the front row, for a hint, or to Miss Liz Saymill for a hint, and play the hand from there. But he made up his mind that if he had to run this funeral he was going to run it his way, and nobody was going to hone his spurs for him.

He said, "Please set down, ma'am. I agree with you, if there's anybody here unfit to face the Lord in His sanctuary, we're going to have an angry God on our hands in about a minute. But the Good Book says, 'Let the women remain quiet in the temple.' So I'll ask the men here to take the necessary steps, and heave out anybody that would offend the Lord, and the only advice I'll give them is what the Savior said on a similar occasion, 'Let him who is without sin cast the first stone!'"

"Amen," somebody said, and somebody else said, "Set down, Stella, you heard him, remain quiet," and somebody else said, "Amen, who is without sin in this town? Nobody, amen!"

Well, Stella knowed she was a one-woman army if she marched out, so she set down, and Mable McMurdoch sneaked into "Lead, Kindly Light," and everybody stood up and whooped that song out from the belly up. Then Rolf led them in a kind of a meandering prayer, searching out the territory you might say, in case Stella Landsdown stood up and heaved another chunk at him, only she didn't. Then they sang, "Up from the Dead He Arose, with a Mighty Triumph O'er His Foes." That's a corker that the average Methodist can't sing, it takes a steam soprano that can go plumb to the top, and you need a couple of men with good deep whisky voices to bleed everything there is out of it. But they done pretty good.

Then Rolf thought he'd gamble a little, and he took his Book of Common Prayer and began reading, "Man, that is born of woman, hath but a short time to live, and is full of misery," and so on. Then he went into his eulogy as he called it, and this is just about what he said, word for word verbatim as the saying is:

"We commit our brother to the judgment of the Lord without judging him ourselves. What we do instead is beseech Him in His mercy to stretch things as fur as He can in favor of this poor fella, because nobody here knows it won't be himself here tomorrow, needing everything that can be said in his favor.

"Colonel Pegler Saymill fought to preserve the Union, and he carried the scars of battle right into that coffin, but he did not carry vengeful hate against his foes, no sir he had nothing but kind words to say about Albert Sidney Johnston, for example.

"He owed no man a dime when he died. He paid in cash as he went along through life, and nobody's loser by his death in that respect.

"He took care of his sister the way a man ought to, and he didn't ask no special credit for it. She was his sister and that was enough for him.

"He claimed he was an atheist, yes he did, but he never tried to talk anybody else out of his faith; if you wanted to believe him, that was up to you, but you really disappointed him if you didn't give him a good lively argument on the subject.

"He drank like a gentleman and was never drunk.

"He seduced no man's innocent daughter or sister, and lusted after no man's wife.

"He consorted with some low-down riffraff, yes he did all right, but so did Jesus when He was here on earth, and Peg Saymill caught criticism for it and I reckon Jesus did too, but enough of that.

"Not many called him friend but nobody called him an enemy either. He lived up to his code, and it was a gentleman's code, and maybe not a Christian code but the next best thing at least.

"So now we consign him to the earth, to become ashes, to become dust, and I who has been in prison tell you this, you can't trust half of the testimony that people are convicted on. There ain't no more Colonel Pegler T. Saymill, we have lost him to God, and this here town is poorer if I'm any judge, and in our poverty and loss, what can we do but pray?"

He cut loose on a prayer that like to ripped the roof off. It added to his confidence to be burying a colonel who had died rich and respected, not some rapist or strangler or horse thief, and he was talking to people that knowed the difference between right and wrong, or at least thought they did. He come down toward the end of the prayer real quiet and friendly and solemn, never whooping or pounding the lectern, and then he give Mable McMurdoch the signal, and she bore down on the pedals and began walloping out "Till We Meet Again, Till We Meet Again, Till We Meet At Jesus's Feet."

He motioned them to stand up, and he hauled off and gave them a benediction, something he hadn't planned on doing at no time, and he got them to filing past the coffin in good order, only he never did catch Abe Whipple's signal to take up a collection. Except for that, it was a mighty well-run funeral, and Colonel Pegler T. Saymill could afford to skip the collection if anybody could.

4

The custom of grave site services hadn't took root in Mooney because the graveyard was so neglected it took the heart out of the strongest believer in the Resurrection, and was uphill besides. Weeds everywhere, and fences down, and prob'ly somebody's milk cow staked out to graze on the graves. Besides it was coming on to rain, with thunder already rolling, and anybody with a lantern wanted to get on home, and not fool around in no graveyard. So Abe deputized four good single men to go with Bernard Petty and get the job done in decent privacy, you might say.

Beatrice Cunningham, who ran Bea's Place over across the crick, waited while everybody else come up to tell Rolf the usual lies, how much they was comforted and so forth. Then she slipped up and interduced herself, and said she prob'ly erred in coming to the obsequies, but it was hard to pass up the funeral of the last true gentleman in town.

Beatrice was about thirty or forty or fifty, with a big pile of yella hair, and nice blue eyes, and she was a well-turned woman as to shape. She used plenty of good French perfume, and you have to remember that Rolf had been two years in the pen away from women, and then had swore off all these things including women.

"I do appreciate the stand you took, Reverend, and I'll never forget it," she said. Rolf just said yuh sure, something like that, and then she said, "I won't embarrass you further, better get in out of the rain, and I'll get across the crick while I still can." He was so strangled on that perfume he hadn't even noticed it was sprinkling good and hard.

Abe was going around with his lantern, telling everybody that Rolf was the former assistant chaplain at the Kansas pen, and not attached to any church, and was a single man, frugal in his tastes. When Rolf went to look for him, to find out where he was going to spend the night, and to get the five dollars from Liz Saymill that Abe had bragged about so free, Abe was just meeting up with this family that had come up in a nice top buggy and had missed the funeral.

"Abe, I just don't understand you going around telling everybody this was a six-hundred-dollar *quarterly* payment," this man was saying. "My business is my business. I regret the tragedy, but it catches me by the short hair; that's a call loan and if the estate calls it, I'm in trouble. And you have to go around telling everybody I have been paying Peg six hundred dollars every *quarter*."

"I didn't get you into debt and I didn't kill Peg, and it'd come out in probate proceedings anyway, Cal," Abe said. "Evidence is evidence, somebody else knowed he had that money; what am I going to do, go around saying it was six bits he died for?"

"I admire your industry," this fella said, "but I wish you had been half as industrious last winter, when I was losing a couple of hundred head of hay-fat cattle."

Abe said, "Now don't start on that; by the way, I want you to meet Reverend Rolf Ledger. Rolf, this is Cal Venaman of the Flying V, and this is his wife Opal, and this is his daughter Sammie, and this is his daughter Winnie."

"Don't call me Sammie," the one girl said.

Now if you had to single out one big family in Mooney, it would be either Cal Venaman of the V, or Alec McMurdoch, president of the State Bank of Mooney and wife of the organist, or husband ruther. Rolf figured the Flying V owner, or the V as they sometimes said, would be a big old raunchy ignorant type, because the cow business wasn't no place for a vanilla salesman in them days. Your average money-making cowman, he had to pull his shirt tail out to tell what day of the week it was, by how dirty it had got since he changed it last Sunday.

But Cal was kind of a gant whippy fella in brown side-whiskers, educated up to the point of college or maybe a little beyond, and usually quite neatly dressed. His wife Opal was a mighty handsome woman, and they made a mighty handsome pair.

The oldest girl, Samantha, had pretty much missed out on the family good looks. Sammie they called her in school, till she put a stop to it when she put her hair up. She was exactly twenty-four years old then, and was as tall as her father, and whippy-built like him, making her too limber of build for a real good-looking woman. She had blue eyes and brown hair almost red, but the thing about Samantha, and this is not an easy thing to say about a woman, was her big mouth. She'd share her opinions with you on short notice, and you didn't have to provoke her to it, all you had to do was be within range.

The younger sister was Winifred, better known as Winnie. Now there was a girl for you. Just seventeen, a head shorter than Samantha, and you talk about built, she was the lonesome cowboy's dream on a cold night, as the fella says. This was the one that Thad Rust was hanging around to his mortal peril. A sweet womanly critter that knowed her place, and none of Samantha's big mouth.

"Ashamed to get here too late for the service, Parson," Cal said, shaking hands, "but we didn't hear of it at all. Are you looking for a charge? You can't say the church is looking for a minister, truthfully. I'm on the board, and it will put off spending a dime for anything as long as possible. But there is a vacancy."

Rolf struck hard and he struck fast, like a diamondback. He said, "No sir, Mr. Venaman, I ain't an ordained preacher, I'm just a cowhand. I was on my way to ask you for a job when I got sidetracked for this."

"An ex-convict, I understand," Cal said.

"Yes sir, pardoned because I wasn't guilty," Rolf said.

"Well," Cal said, "I wouldn't necessarily hold that against you, but I'm afraid I couldn't use you. On the Flying V, I'm the sole source of the gospel. No, I couldn't risk a rival moral leader, to be quite frank."

Abe said, "Well it's sure been nice talking to you folks; don't rush into anything, Cal, we still got to talk over who's going to fill this pulpit someday."

"You're the one rushing things," Cal said. "Why can't we chat a moment with the parson?"

"Because it's going to rain is why," Abe said.

"It'll rain on the just and the unjust as usual, Abe. I only wish you was half as conscientious about what happened to my livestock as you are in finding a preacher for the First Methodist Church," Cal said.

Abe mopped his face with his sleeves, and said, "Cal, if you couldn't track your steers through the Goddamn snow, excuse that, ladies, how do you expect me to do it in spring grass? You don't bother to get out and rustle around in a storm, oh no indeedy, you're too comfortable there by the fire rubbing your sock feet against each other! Well a cow thief can't take things so easy. He's got to ply his trade when he can, and then you can only think to blame the law enforcement officers."

Cal had already stopped listening to him in that highhanded way he had, and as soon as he could, he said, "Parson, are you interested in this church?"

"Not in any way, shape, or form," Rolf said.

Abe said, "Now wait a minute!" But Cal slid in between his words and his ideas, and he said, "My feeling is that your experience in prison would be more useful in the pulpit than in a crew on a working ranch. I've worked a few ex-convicts. They were all unjustly convicted, and they're hard people to get a day's work out of."

Rolf said, "Well, you do lose your touch with a horse or rope, after fondling a sledge hammer a few years. But I reckon I'll make out when I land me a job."

"You might try a neighbor of mine, Jack Butler," Cal said. "It's a one-man outfit, and Jack has no moral boundaries that I've ever discerned."

Abe said, "Cal, do you mean you suspicion Jack of running off your steers?"

"You've got more sense than that. No neighbor ran them off one at a time. They were driven north in a herd. I sent a man to get Jack to help us track them, but he was laying drunk, I won't mention where, and had been for three days. But he needs a man if he can afford one, and an ex-convict may not be too particular about bachelor cooking and the suspense of waiting for Jack to go on one of his periodic toots," Cal said.

"It may be an idee at that, Cal," Abe said. "Reverend Ledger could help him fight his fiend, and Jack's place is close enough so he could get in here Sundays to preach."

"I ain't going to preach and I ain't got any patience with drunks," Rolf said.

It was still making up to rain, showering every now and

then, but Cal and Abe went on talking and paying no attention to him. Cal said it would amuse him to see a man of real experience with sin and suffering in the pulpit, and Abe said that was exactly his own idee, and Cal said preaching wasn't a lazy man's job in *this* town, and Abe said no, it sure wasn't if it was done right.

Samantha spoke up and said, "Reverend Ledger, before I form an opinion, how do you stand on the theory of evolution?"

"Darwin, you mean?" Rolf said.

She snapped, "Do you know any other theory of evolution?"

Rolf said, "No, but for all I know there could be a dozen. The chaplain in prison gave me one of Darwin's books to read, and he explained it to me later. Darwin's a little foggy to push through, but if you don't let go too easy, he can be read."

She said, "Well, are you for or against it?"

Rolf said, "How can you be for or against it? Either it happened or it didn't, it ain't like getting out the vote to close the saloons, we're talking about backwards, not forwards, you might as well vote on a comet."

"You evade the question. Do you or do you not believe in the theory of evolution?" Samantha said.

Rolf kind of walled his eyes like a bronc being pushed into the saddling chute, and he tried to hold it in but she had savaged him just a little too hard. He said it was an insulting question and if she was a man, he'd tell her it was none of her business. Cal said, "Sickem, wolf, go to it, bulldog!" He had come out loser in too many arguments with Samantha himself.

"Do you or do you *not*?" Samantha said.

Rolf said, "I'm a workingman, and I don't believe in it the way I do low prices and high wages. Them things make a difference to me. Since the wheat farmers plowed up the range from Texas to Saskatoon, a workingman has got more to worry about than whether his ancestors was apes or ant-eaters. You go up there in the Black Hills and see men working twelve hours a day in them gold mines for a dollar and a half, and coming out with no fingers, or their eye put out, or deefened

by careless blasting for life, where did I leave off? Them is
the things that count with me. Whether they come down from
apes, and before that lizards, and before that some kind of
jelly fish, today they're breaking their rear ends for a dollar
and a half. Or you take the railroads; now these automatic
couplers is supposed to make railroading safe as clerking dry
goods, but how about the cars that's still link-and-pin? Them
highbinders ain't going to burn all them old man-killing cars!
I seen a man that stepped in between two cars to link up, and
his foot slipped, and you should of seen him after that link
went through his meat in the middle. I'll tell you what, ma'am,
he didn't care a whoop about his remote ancestors, all he
wished was it had cut his backbone so he could die easy, and
I'd feel the same way. So when you ask about evolution, I
say how about outlawing link-and-pin today, instead of after
them death-trap ancient cars wear out! Now there was a certain kind of a bird Professor Darwin seen on some island, and
it was almost the same as the same kind of a brown bird he
seen somewhere else, except he claimed that natural selection
had changed a few little things. That was interesting, sure it
was, laying in a cell in prison with nothing to think about except how I got there, and how I was going to get out, and if
Professor Darwin himself was to come up right now and ask
me if I was for him or against him, I'd tell him he's just making a nuisance of himself. What I want to do is make a living.
The same with transubstantiation, now if you want to believe
that way it's all right with me, or if you're for consubstantiation instead, that's all right with me too, just show me where
I can get a job to make an honest living. But if you insist that
I've got to pick between the two, then I've got to say that I
just don't *know*. And if you ask me what was my practice as
the assistant chaplain in prison, why, I'll serve out the wafer
and the wine to all comers, and I only wish that the transub-
stantiationists and the consubstantiationists and the evolution-
ists had to make a few couplings with link-and-pin on a dark
track on a wet night, or you look at life on a cow outfit for the
hired hand, how many men have you seen going around with

a limp from being throwed or walked on by a horse, or with a finger tore off at the roots by a rope, or— Where was I? Oh yes, evolution."

He catched his breath, and Samantha just stared at him like she had swallowed a frog, but that woman had the doubtful gift of a ready tongue. She said, "I don't think that's sound Methodist doctrine or any other kind of doctrine I ever heard of. Not that I care! I believe in evolution, and I'm only glad I don't have to compromise my beliefs, well look at it rain, so nice to of met you, Reverend, we must have another chat sometime."

It was coming down in bucketfuls. The Venamans run to their buggy and got the side curtains up, and Abe and Rolf started for town. Abe said, "I want you to talk to Jack Butler, and he's laying drunk in the Jackrabbit if he hasn't come out of it, and tomorrow the crick may be too high to cross. So come on."

Rolf wasn't anxious to talk to no drunks about a job, and he wasn't about to let this sheriff run his life for him. But you might as well holler down your stove pipe, or up it, as argue with Abe Whipple when he had one of his enthusiasms going.

There was a big cottonwood log forty inches thick across the crick, with the top adzed flat, and an old rope for a handrail that went out with every high water, and stayed out until somebody found some more old rope and strung it up. This was all the bridge there was, and the rigs had to go a quarter of a mile up the crick to the ford. The water was still normal when they crossed.

It being come on to rain, you wouldn't expect a crowd in the Jackrabbit, but the shooting of Colonel Pegler T. Saymill had brought folks to town, and a storm was all the excuse they needed. A couple of the Jackrabbit girls shook their tails at Rolf, but Abe said, "Goddamn it, this man is a minister of the gospel!" One of the girls said she had problems with her soul and was willing to exchange blessings, but Abe told her to get the hell out or he would be forced to jail her a few days.

"How do you know, maybe I could help her with her problems," Rolf said.

"Not the one she's got," Abe said.

"How do you know?" Rolf said.

"I thought you swore off!" Abe said.

"I did, but life goes on, and it ain't life without a few things. Maybe at your age, but not mine," Rolf said.

Abe just about boiled up, but then he seen that Rolf was just making fun of him. Rolf said, "We'll keep the Commandments, Sheriff, but don't make up my mind for me! I'll tell you something else, the chaplain said that for every fallen woman, there's some man that pushed her, and maybe that girl does need help."

"There's some that was pushed," the sheriff said, "and some that fell, and some that just laid down. Some things you can advise me about, Reverend, but not that."

They sent a girl to call Huey, and they both turned down a free drink on the house, even strawberry syrup in water, Rolf because of his vows and the position he was in after preaching a funeral, and Abe because a woman had put knockout drops in his cherry water once in San Francisco, and took his poke away from him. They'll do that in San Francisco every time.

Huey come in, and Abe told him to go get Jack Butler. He grumbled somewhat, but he went down into his cellar and brought Jack up. "A good thing, too," he said, "because the water is rising down there. Welcome back to life and Lickety Split, Jack."

"Oh God oh God oh God oh God," Jack said.

"You may well say that, you sot, you miserable whisky fiend, you hopeless drunkard," Abe said.

"Oh God oh God," Jack said.

"How about a drink to damp your fuse?" Huey said.

"It would kill me," Jack said. "One taste would stop my heart. Oh God oh God oh God."

Jack Butler was about forty-five years old, give or take a few years. When sober he was just a plain decent-looking fella, usually a very serious expression, not very big and not very small, just like any old batch of forty-five that minded his own business. But coming out of a bout with his demon, like tonight, he wanted to puke and couldn't, and had the look in his eye like he'd been scraped out of the saddle when he let his horse run under a low limb.

Abe give him a good talking-to, and the Jackrabbit girls brought him black coffee and peeled raw potatoes, which he always craved coming out of one. He tried to pull his mind together, to keep it from tracking all over. Abe told him he wanted him to hire Rolf for twenty-five dollars a month, and Jack said, "A man can't make a decision like that in my shape, Abe, so let's put it off. I know you're looking out for my interests, but—"

Abe said, "Don't you bet on that, Jack. I can lose patience with you mighty fast. You're going to give him Saturday afternoon off, so he can scratch a sermon together for Sunday, and a good horse so he can make it here and back."

"I ain't going to preach no sermon," Rolf said. But Abe didn't pay no attention to him, and he kept on until Jack said sure, he could use a good man if he didn't mind batching, and he'd let him use Fanny to go in to conduct the Methodist services. That was a brown mare, four years old, three white stockings and a narrow blaze on her face, that he just doted on, and rightfully.

"It may be just what I need, Abe," Jack said. "Maybe the reverend can help me with my problem too."

"Nobody can help a drunk but himself," Rolf said.

"You never spoke truer words," Abe said, "but at least you won't lead this pitiful son of a bitch into temptation. Look what this will mean to the county!

"Why, an ex-convict, the former assistant chaplain in a prison, comes riding up to the church every Sunday on the prettiest little gaited mare you ever seen, to preach to his flock. Same time, it comes out that I'm part Sephardic Spanish Jew. You said it yourself—people like to be different. We'll be the standout county in Colorado!"

Rolf said he wasn't going to preach nowhere, and Abe might

as well brag his ancestors was monkeys, and so on. There's something about a saloon that just about makes it impossible to end a conversation without starting a fight, and Little Dick Silver kept wandering in and out, and he could distract them if anybody could, and he did. Dick was an old Army scout, and he wore his white hair in long curls down over his shoulders, and a big white mustache and goatee, and stayed drunk a good part of the time, and couldn't be trusted with a pistol any time. He had went out on the prairie and picked some pink and white Sweet Williams, and he went around handing everybody flowers and saying, "The message I bring is loving kindness for everybody free of charge," and finely Abe had to tell him where he could put his Sweet Williams.

"There's a little thing called ordination, Sheriff," Rolf said. "I ain't ordained and I ain't going to be ordained, and you can't preach unless you are."

Abe said, "That could be a poser except I'm sure it's a legal technicality. I'll talk to Jimmy Drummond about it, and if there's a better lawyer on these technical propositions, I ain't heard of him. The way I look at it, I can't swear in a regular deputy without the county commissioners authorizing it in an ordinance, and they're so mean and stingy that look at what I can afford, Thad Rust, a well-meaning boy, but too prone to fire his weapon, and he couldn't handle a hen-house robbery alone.

"But in an emergency, I swear in a *posse comitatus,* on my own authorization, and I lead them out to make an arrest or a corpse as circumstances provide, and any court in the country will back me to the hilt. I look on this as a similar emergency. Why can't we have a preacher *comitatus?* A divine militia you might say, keeping the spiritual peace in the absence of the regular ordained troops.

"It don't stand to reason you've got to leave a pulpit empty in an emergency, waiting for somebody to blunder along that's been ordained. What if the Lord Himself came back for His Second Coming, and didn't have the papers to prove He was ordained, why He couldn't even take the pulpit to talk to a few Methodists that was already all for Him! Or they say they are. Sometimes I just wonder."

"An empty pulpit and a full saloon, they're the brand and earmark of a backwards town," Jack Butler said. "A preacher *comitatus*, well say, Abe, you sure do come up with some fertile ideas. But it may hold water at that."

5

At least Rolf had himself a job, so as soon as Jack Butler could set on a horse with a reasonable hope of not swooning off'n it, they went out to his place, the J Bar B, and it was a real pleasant surprise to Rolf. Jack had himself a shelf up in the hills, with timber and water in addition to grass. Not a big spread, but you couldn't of told it from the best parts of Wyoming, and you can't say no more for cow country.

Jack didn't have much of a herd, but what he had was good-looking brood cows, and bulls of the whiteface persuasion. But he had the best fences Rolf ever seen, fences across draws that snowed in during the winter and could starve cattle, and fences around hayfields that he cut for winter feed, and fences that kept his cows out of Cal Venaman's grass and Flying V cows out of his'n.

He had a nice three-room log house without a draft in it, and a fireplace for heat and a cookstove to cook on, and nice big mattresses on the beds, not just straw ticks, and plenty of chairs that didn't teeter, and even curtains on the windows.

"They're scrim," Jack said. "I sent off to the mail order for them, and Mrs. Bloodgood at the post office helped me make out the order, and she said scrim was the thing."

"Scrim. Well you learn something every day," Rolf said. "Looks to me like you're putting everything you make back into your property, and in time your natural increase will make you a rich man."

"I hope so," Jack said, "but it ain't planning, Rolf. I spend it for bobwire and things before I can spend it for drink, in case a fit comes on me."

"It would be a blessing if your fight against the drink made you a rich man," Rolf said. "The Lord moves in a mysterious way, His wonders to perform."

"Well," Jack said, "the first thing, we've got to haul some more bobwire from Fort Morgan. I already got more bobwire than I know what to do with, but I ordered this when I felt a fit coming on last winter, and I waited a mite too late, and was already drunk. I knowed there was something I meant to do, so when I remembered what it was, I done it, so I sure am going to be well fixed for bobwire."

They et their supper together real pleasant. Like most cowboys, Jack was a pretty good cook with beans and oatmeal and bacon and the like, and Rolf had worked in the prison kitchen and knowed a few fancy tricks himself. There was not going to be any problem about food.

The next morning, Rolf hooked up a four-horse team before daylight, and took along some cold beans and some bacon sandwiches in biscuits, and a bottle of coffee, and headed for Fort Morgan. He got there and lo and behold, here was a whole carload of bobwire. Now that's just a mountain of bobwire. When Rolf got his load on, just spool after spool of it, he seen he hadn't hardly made a dent in that load.

He got back about dark, and Jack told him to unload behind the stone barn, and when Rolf pulled around behind the stone barn, there was a stack of bobwire almost as high as the stone barn. Rolf asked him how in the world he expected to use all of it, and Jack said, "I don't know what you can do with it except build fence, I honestly don't. But look at all the liquor that would of bought."

"You're going to have your place fenced horse-high, hog-tight, and bull-strong, as the fella says. You could fence yourself away from all the liquor in the world with the bobwire you got here," Rolf said.

Jack said, "Rolf, I could climb a red-hot fence a mile high, barefoot and blindfolded, if you tell me where a bottle is hid when I've got a thirst on me. Don't poke fun at a man's weakness."

Rolf was three weeks hauling that bobwire, and he tore his hands up a little, but he made some muscle too. In the pen he had learned how to be alone without getting fidgety and vile-tempered from lonesomeness, and mostly he sort of lined up arguments in his mind in case him and Samantha Venaman ever butted heads again on a question of theology. He had her hobbled and belled and blindfolded every time, as a man will when it's all in his head, and he could just picture her apologizing for putting her female arguments up against his'n.

Now all this whole three weeks he was hauling bobwire, he didn't so much as mention going to Mooney to preach, and neither did Jack, and neither did Sheriff Abe Whipple come out to make an issue of it. At first Rolf figgered he had wore that old sheriff out, but Jack said you never could trust Abe Whipple, just when he ort to be throwing in his hand, here he comes tilting the pot like he had aces back to back. He was that kind of a man, Jack said, crafty as an old dog-coyote, and could wait with his nose in a rabbit hole as long as it took to get him that rabbit.

After he finished hauling the wire, Rolf plowed up a potato patch, and then started planting some potatoes so they wouldn't have to depend on beans all the time next winter. He was planting away when he seen a nice top buggy coming, pulled by two nice matched bays, at a nice easy canter. Now nobody owned that kind of a rig but Cal Venaman, and when he made out three female figgers in it, it didn't take no brains to speak of to know it was Opal and her two girls, Samantha and Winnie. Their place was only six miles cross-country from Jack's, or eight by wagon road, with only one gate to open.

Samantha was driving. She flourished up to where Rolf was

planting potatoes, and Opal give him a nice smile, and said, "Reverend Ledger, my girls and I have a surprise for you and Jack."

"Please don't call me reverend, ma'am," Rolf said.

"Take note I didn't," Samantha said.

"Now, Samantha!" Opal said. "Sammie beat up a sponge last night, and she got up this morning early, and rolled out the dough and made some real nice light rolls. Then we thought of you two lonely bachelors, and we decided while they're fresh we'd bring you some."

She fetched out a big pan of nice light rolls from under the seat, and whipped off the dish towel over them, and held them out to him, and said, "Just smell that!" Rolf leaned over and smelled them, and he thanked her and said there was nothing on earth, not even roses, that smelled as good as fresh bread.

Winnie said, "We brought you some butter, too, see? From our own press." She showed him the round pound of butter, with the Flying V in the middle and a row of braided design around the edge. Having your own butter press with your own brand is something most cowmen wouldn't bother with, because in the first place not many cowmen milk cows, let alone make butter, and in the second, your own hand-carved hardwood press could cost you as much as three or four dollars in Denver.

"Well say, ladies," Rolf said, "you're going to have us two batches just crying our eyes out from pure gratitude."

Samantha said, "I've made better bread in my time, and I'd be ashamed if I couldn't, but it won't poison you. Just don't make hogs of yourselves. You know how heavy fresh bread lays on your stomach."

"Not this kind, ma'am," Rolf said. "This would be as light as butterflies on your stomach."

So far they was doing fine, passing the peace pipe around in good shape, and burying the hatchet too. Only just then Jack Butler ambled up in his gum boots, from where he had been mucking out the horse barn, and was enough to kill anybody's appetite.

"Fresh light bread!" he said. "Too bad you had to bring them today, right after Rolf made us some yesterday. You talk about light-bread buns, these is mighty good homemade ones, but homemade ain't in it with the way Rolf learned in prison."

Opal's eyes bugged out, and she got red-faced, and she started laughing and whooping, until it was all she could do to say, "You mean Reverend Ledger can bake?"

"The best," Jack said. "He says that when you can bake for the warden's family, the only better job in the pen is assistant to the chaplain."

"Well I declare," Opal said, and she just leaned back and let herself go. But Samantha said, "Mama, don't be entirely an undignified idiot. You'll recall I was against the whole idea, I said it was a waste of time, casting our pearls before swine."

"I don't know as that's fair now," Rolf said.

"Fair or unfair, I'll scatter that bread in the timber for the deer first!" Samantha said.

Well Rolf's mane crested a little, and he said, "Don't pick on the poor helpless deer, ma'am, us swine will take care of these pearls, as you say."

Opal just laughed until she cried. She said, "Well I never seen two workingmen who couldn't work their way through two batches of light bread; just bring the pan back sometime when you're riding our way. And if you want to fill them with Reverend Ledger's light-bread buns, that will be fine with me."

"Mama, you infuriate me," Samantha said.

"Because you have no funny bone," Opal said. "Oh dear, we'll never live this down."

"I'll see to it that you don't," Samantha said.

Jack said, "Remind Cal he was going to put that off mare to his black stud. I do believe she's coming in, and what he wanted was a spring colt."

Samantha let out a bleat, "Pet—Lottie— Git!" She cracked the whip over the team, and out of the yard they went.

Rolf said, "Jack, that was about the most ignorant thing you could of said."

"Why, I used to own Lottie myself," Jack said. "I raised her

out of a mare I traded an Indian out of, let's see, Willie Bonfire
was his name, her sire was half mustang and half Kentucky
hotblood. Cal had this mare he called Pet, a perfect mate for
my filly—"

You get Jack on a horse story, and the dam has broke, and
you're up on the ridgepole, and you could fire a cannon between his feet and he'd never lose his grip on where he was in
the horse story.

"I don't mean about the horse coming in heat," Rolf said. "I
mean letting on we already had fresh bread."

"Well we did," Jack said.

"Jack, do you know what a gentleman is?" Rolf said. "I
heard this from the chaplain; a gentleman is somebody that
never *unintentionally* causes pain."

"How does he know if it's unintentional?" Jack said.

"That's the whole point. Think, Jack, think!" Rolf said.

Jack thought, and said, "It's too deep for me. You can swear
off'n intentional things, I can see that, but the other is too much
to ask of human flesh; you might as well swear off'n unintentional sneezing, or unintentional farting, or unintentional
yawning. I'd like you to show me in the Bible where that is
about what a gentleman is. I bet that ain't the whole verse."

That was how Jack Butler was, if you let him he could drive
you crazy, and you might as well hang yourself in advance as
to be snowed in with him, but Rolf could get away from him
now and then, and get his bearings, so he didn't feel he was
on a runaway merry-go-round listening to Jack talk.

The trouble was, Jack really didn't need a hand, just somebody to amuse him so he wouldn't fall into drink. But with all
that bobwire, there was no excuse for not building fence, so
that's what they done. Building fence ain't a bad job, if you
don't get too much of it at once, because a short stretch of
fence gives you a nice change. First you go out and cut your
posts. Then you hitch up your team and haul your posts to
where you're going to string your fence, and you lay them out
in a line. Then you dig your holes, and you've got to set your
posts right away, so some critter don't step in the empty hole

and break his leg. Then you get the stretchers out and hang your top bobwire. Then you go along and steeple it down. Then you hang the next wire, and so on, until you've got as many wires as you need, or as you can afford.

But where you're stringing a long fence, first you've got all post-cutting, and then all post-hauling, and then all post-setting, and then nothing but stretching your wire day after day. And Jack Butler lost a lot of his charm after you'd heard his stories a few times. Most of them was horse stories, with a few mules throwed in for variety, and a couple of famous poker hands he had seen, and a reformed train robber he had met, and a woman who picked his pocket in Kansas City. He had a couple of stories about widows he had courted, but he said they wasn't the kind you'd ordinarily tell a preacher, and Rolf didn't give him no encouragement.

Jack came to feel the same way about Rolf and his life in prison, until one evening he said, "Rolf, I don't know about you, but I need a change from yarns about prisoners cutting each other with spoon handles they sharpened on the stone floor, and betting who can find the most worms in the salt pork, and so on. I'm frank with my friends, and I consider you a friend, and I'd appreciate knowing how you feel about it."

Rolf said, "Jack, spoken like a man! I swore off the liquor, but you can drive me so close to drink with your same old stories that I can understand your weakness for it. I think you drive yourself to drink with them stories of yours."

"You see, we're getting on each other's nerves! I say let's go to Mooney," Jack said.

Rolf squinted at him and said, "And get drunk, you mean? Do you feel a thirst coming on?"

"Oh Lord no!" Jack said. "Just for a change, before we come to blows and you force me to kill you."

"I'm sorry to disappoint you on that score," Rolf said, "but you won't kill me. I learned to fight before I went to prison, and I learned more after I was in there, and I'd have you picking up your own guts before you could trip on them."

"That's what you think," Jack said, "but this only proves it's time to go to Mooney and see somebody else than each other for a change."

So they saddled up and rode in, the first time Jack had let Rolf ride this Fanny mare, the most beautiful little mare he had ever rode, and only five years old. By the time they got to Mooney, Rolf was so enchanted with her, he was even considering preaching. The only thing he could fault her with, he wished she had four white feet instead of three. And like he said, that was pure vanity, that was criticizing the Lord's judgment in one of His finest creations. Next to a pure woman, you've got to rank an innocent child as the Lord's best work, but a good horse ain't going to be fur behind in third place, even ahead of a good hunting dog or a lifelong friend.

They put their horses in the livery barn on the respectable side of the crick, and Jack went over to Lickety Split, and Rolf went into a store and bought a nickel's worth of candy corn and a pair of socks, and then just about every other amusement in town was ruled out by his vows. He walked up and down the streets watching the dogfights, and a drunk who was fishing a penny out of a crack in the plank sidewalk, and a rooster that was scaring himself to death on top of an upside-down washtub. Every time he'd haul off to crow, he'd have to flap his wings, and when he whanged the tub with them wings it would boom out and scare him cross-eyed. The minute he got over it he'd try it again, but he never did get to where he could let out a crow. He'd get his neck craned and his beak open, and then BOOM, BOOM, BOOM he'd thump that washtub with his wings, and he'd jump a foot in the air and come down cross-eyed. Finely he had to give up, and he slunk off looking like he'd swore off ever crowing again, and he went into the blacksmith shop, and then under a tree where it was shady, and he stood there shaking his head for a long time.

A young fella figuring on what his life's work is going to be, he ought to consider how he'll spend his time off. A blacksmith or anybody that works with his muscle, he can put his feet up on another chair, and he don't need to read or think or nothing, and if he's got a couple of days off, why fishing is tailor-made, he don't care whether they bite or not. A storekeeper can go to Denver or Cheyenne or San Antonio or Sioux Falls, and let his wife go to concerts, and have wine with his supper, and maybe slip away from her for a couple of hours while she's trying on corsets. Or a liveryman can take a hotel room, as far from horses as he can get, and have the bellboy bring up a bottle, and a couple of sporting newspapers, and some cigars, and he don't need anything else. But what is a preacher going to do when he gets some time off? If he ever does.

So it came to where Rolf thought he had better look Jack up before he yielded to temptation, so he clumb down the crick bank and went over on the foot log, and he seen Jack right away, setting in Bea Cunningham's front parlor, drinking coffee with her where they could watch across the crick in case there was anything to see. She tapped on the window and said, "Come in, Reverend Ledger, I'm sure you won't do your future prospects in Mooney any good, but Abe Whipple and Jimmy Drummond are looking for you. They said they'd be back."

Rolf said he had just come to check up on Jack, and she said Jack would never get a drop on her premises. So he set down and had a cup of coffee with her and Jack, and pretty soon Abe showed up with this lawyer. He said it saved him a long ride out to the J Bar B, and this was as good a place as any to get things straight.

Rolf liked this Jimmy Drummond right off. Jimmy Drummond was a fairly old man, and he spent his time working or reading, and there wasn't much legal business for him in a town the size of Mooney, but his wife was buried there and he reckoned he'd stay to lie beside her in the end. He said:

"Abe's problem is one I've been prepared to deal with for years, and never expected to. I read law in a firm whose senior partner spent his life in research on the subject. He wrote a treatise that will never be published, because it isn't litigated as often as you may think. Religion causes a lot of arguments, but you'd be surprised how few times it gets into court."

"I wouldn't," Rolf said. "Any time you settle a religious argument, you take all the fun out of it."

"True, true," Jimmy said. "I can tell you what I think, based on a unique work in the history of law."

He had this fellow's life's work with him, a stack of paper six inches high, that he had entitled *Principles of Ecclesiastical Law,* and he had been through it from front to back, and had threshed out a few kernels that might be called wisdom or might be just weed seeds, depending on your point of view.

He said, "Of course the surest method is that of consecration by consecrated authority, to wit, a bishop or authority of equal rank. But the Congregationals don't have bishops, and they developed the system of ordaining by laying on of hands by the congregation, or by board members, deacons, elders, or vestrymen. There is also ordination by convention, when a candidate is examined publicly in faith and doctrine, or certified as reliable by a legally constituted examining board, after which the convention votes his ordination."

And so on. Or you could get yourself a Bible and go out and free-lance, and nobody could stop you from calling yourself Reverend, and the state would recognize marriages you performed, because the state wasn't going to get itself into no cat-fights about ordination, no sir, if it satisfied the married parties, it satisfied the state. Or you could go to a college, or for that matter start your own college, and along with your diploma you got ordained, and from that minute you was free to tote the light unto the Gentiles.

But Jimmy said, "I think the best thing for this young man is for the board to examine him in faith and doctrine, and lay on their hands, and declare him ordained, and then send the record of the procedure to the bishop. This isn't a two-bit congregation, and if the Methodists fool around too long, the Congregationalists or the Babtists or the Lutherans or somebody is going to step in here and take over a going concern, and the bishop knows that as well as anybody. Now that's what I would do, if I was you."

"Well thanks," Rolf said, "but you went to a lot of trouble for nothing. Nobody's going to examine me and nobody's going to lay any hands on me, and that's that. I've got a good job punching cows, and that suits me."

"Building fence, you mean," Abe said. "What a way for a good horseman to make a living! Why do you think I let you alone out there all these weeks, why, to come to your senses is why, punching cows my eye, you've forgot how to saddle a horse."

They jawed it over for a while, but Rolf's mind was made up, and finely the sheriff got up and clamped on his hat and went out, and Bea said, "I never saw Abe in such a state. It means a lot to him to get a preacher for that church. He's wiser than you may think. Discord in a church is a serious thing. It can wreck a town."

"I hate to see it happen myself," Jimmy Drummond said. "Of course I haven't got the stake in it that you have, an investment like you have in this place, I mean."

Bea said she wished Rolf would change his mind, and he said he wouldn't, and she seen his mind was made up so she let him alone.

6

Rolf seen that Jack was not in immediate peril of drownding his sorrows, so he started back to the other side of the town, but on the way he picked up a nice soft white-pine stick somebody had dropped, so he set down to whittle and think on the crick bank. He was just going good when here came old Abe Whipple looking for him again.

Abe said, "Listen, Reverend, we've got about as pitiful a case over there with one of the Jackrabbit girls as you ever seen. Her name is Lois. To make a long story short, she hasn't been at the Jackrabbit very long, but already she's one of his most famous girls. There was a fella come all the way from Greeley today to see her, based entirely on what he'd heard. He should of had better sense, naturally, and I won't go into details with you, but some of the things he heard about her is just an absolute impossibility.

"He brought along fifty dollars, a princely sum for even a Jackrabbit girl. Now here's the tragedy, Reverend. The minute they met, it turns out he's her brother, and she's his baby sister that he ain't seen since she was twelve years old back in Cincinnati. Almighty God, you can imagine the shame. It throwed her into a convulsion, just the pure shame of it. Doc Nobile says she'll die of it."

"What happened to the brother?" Rolf said.

"He went out the back door, right across there not more than a hundred yards, you could see it if it wasn't for the brush and Huey's privy, and he took a knife and cut his own throat. He made a bad mess of it, but he got the main job done all right, it killed him deader than hell. The thing is, even if this girl comes out of the convulsion, they've got to tell her about her brother, and she'll prob'ly flop right back into it again."

"Why are you telling me this?" Rolf said.

"Well, Dr. Nobile calls it catatonic hysteria, and he says it's beyond medical aid. He said you might have a chance to fetch her up," Abe said.

"What does she look like?" Rolf said.

"Reverend, she's just stiff as a board, with her eyes walled back to the whites, and her eyelids only half open, and my God you ought to see her mouth! It's like a grin only no grin you ever seen before, more like a wolf that has died hard from strychnine."

Rolf said, "I seen a prisoner go catatonic once, only he didn't stiffen up. He got limp as a rag, and he just tapered off breathing until he quit entirely."

"I reckon it's different with a woman, they must get stiff as a board. Doc Nobile says it's a sickness of the soul, and you're a better physician than he is for it. That's quite an admission for a medical man to make. I'd say it checks the bet to you."

Rolf shook his head slowly and went on whittling. "No, Abe. I know my powers and I ain't ashamed of them. I've got guts enough to bury a man, or forgive his sins, or lead a Sabbath chapel lesson. But there's a thing called a 'call,' and either you feel it or you don't, and I don't. And if I was the Lord, and somebody I hadn't called turned up trying to heal somebody in My name, I'd consider he had took a lot onto himself."

Abe laid his hand on Rolf's shoulder and said, "I see what you mean, but listen, I went to look for you at Beatrice Cunningham's place first, and she said tell you this. She says she *knows* you have the power to heal this girl. She says you can give her back her life, her pride, her hope, and her soul. She says *she* can get along without a soul, but it's plain that Lois can't. She said to tell you that, Reverend. You know as well as I do that you're not going to get any spurious spiritual talk from a madam in a whorehouse, this woman says she *knows*, because she's seen it in your eyes whether you feel it's there or not. Maybe you can argue with her, Reverend, but I'm older than you, and by God I can't."

Rolf leaned down and rested his forehead on his hand, and done his best to think of a decent way to get out of it, not because he was afraid of the job, but because he was satisfied with the way things was and he didn't want to risk any change in his life. But there wasn't no way he could talk himself out of it, he had to go see that girl and do his best.

So he put his pine stick away where he could find it again, and closed up his jackknife, and him and Abe went over to the Jackrabbit. They had laid this girl out on her bed of sin, on her back, and had took off her shoes and hair net. She had a crucifix hanging around her neck by a chain, and Rolf thought sure she was a Catholic, but one of the other girls said no, Lois won that in a crap game with a fellow from Idaho only last night.

This girl was so white she was blue, like she had been washed with bluing in the water, and her mouth was just like

Abe said, more a snarl than a smile, and you couldn't see her breathe. Jack Butler broke out sobbing the minute he seen her. There wasn't no way you could keep that man out of something like that.

"I wish I had brought a Bible along," Rolf said. "This will be like dealing with my eyes shut. Well, the rest of you get out of here and lock the door."

They seen him kneel down before they closed the door, and Huey said, "What good will it do to save this poor little whore? How else can she make a living? She can't sew or cook or raise garden or chickens, and this just about disables her for the trade. Some people sure have tough luck in this life."

"Shut up and bow your Goddamn head," Abe said, so he did, and they all shut up and listened. It was a mighty thin door, which ought to be a good lesson to anybody goes into one of those places thinking he's got any privacy to speak of. They could only hear a word here and a word there, and at first Rolf wasn't praying at all, he was just kneeling down there talking to this girl with his mouth to her ear, in a nice soft voice.

He told her the Lord Himself when He walked the earth had a mighty good friend by the name of Mary Magdalene who was in the same business, and He just gave her one good straight look, and she was new and white and clean like she'd just been born. He said there was another hooker that fixed herself up by just reaching out and touching the hem of His shirttail. He told her she might think she didn't deserve a friend left in the world, but he was going to be her friend, and Jesus would be her friend too, and anybody that mistreated her would have them both to account to.

He said life was a tough old trail to ride for poor folks, and she had spent her whole life getting into this fix, true enough. But he said there was savages all over the world *born* in worse shape than she was, and the Lord held out His arms to them. He said he had seen the Canadian Indians hire their daughters out when they was only nine or ten years old, but they was still children, and of such was the Kingdom of Heaven. He said the Lord would put His arm around them when the time came and never think He wouldn't. He said that in China, they throwed girl babies into the river to drownd them, or else they raised them to be ten or eleven and sold them to be whores in the seaports, and at least her folks hadn't done that to her.

He said that when she got stiff as a board it was trying to punish herself for her sins, and that wasn't none of her business at all, Judgment is mine saith the Lord, and who do you think you are? Throwing around the wrath of God like you was God Himself, when them kids in China had it a lot worse than she ever had! He said he had seen men in prison, so vile and miserable that she was pure as an angel compared to them, a whorehouse wasn't half as bad as prison if only people knowed what went on there, and he could testify that the power of the Lord got through them steel doors anyway, and every now and then brought somebody to his senses in time, and he'd seen it happen. Not to mention any names, he said, he knowed one prisoner that was just about the stubbornest fool he had ever met, and the Lord didn't let *him* down, in fact this fellow was pardoned soon after.

He said the Lord cautioned people about being stiff-necked, and here she was being stiff all over, when all she had to do was let herself go limp and feel the arm of Jesus go around her. He said that it was sure enough true that Jesus hated sin, but He loved sinners, and if He could meet her, all He'd say was, "Lois, go and sin no more!"

Well at this she started to breathe so a man could see it, and he kept on talking to her, and then he seen her eyes unwall, so the dark part showed as well as the whites. Then she began to cry, and then to scream, and he thought he was going to have to slap her to keep her from going stiff on him again.

But he just said, "All right, you're limbered up again, now here's what I want you to do. I want you to get down on your knees and pray for peace of mind and heart and soul."

She said, "Oh bullshit, my own brother, he always took such pride in the family, and in me, he used to bring me paper flowers and kerchiefs and things when he come back from his trips, I say bullshit to you."

He said that was fine with him, if that was the way she felt about him. But he said, "I'll tell you one thing, you've got more guts than your brother had. Your brother is dead."

She said she knew it, she knew it, oh my God he killed himself. Rolf said, "Yes he did, and what you and me can only guess at, he knows now. Maybe there's no heaven, and no hell, nothing but cold meat when we die. If you know that, then go ahead and do it your way, but I sure don't, and if I's you, I'd look at the other side for a change. Just in case it turned out there *was* a heaven, and there *was* forgiveness, and there *was* a merciful God who forgave the sinner. I'd try to picture your no-account brother up there trying to square himself fast—not because he's afraid of burning up in hell forever, *but for your sake!* I don't see how you can take a chance, Lois, because what if he is up there trying to do something for you, and you're down here refusing even to say a prayer."

He wore her out, or something, because she did get down and pray, but she couldn't think of no words. Rolf said he'd do the praying, and all she had to do was let out an "amen" every time something went past her that she agreed with.

Abe reckoned now was the time for them to get out of there, so him and Huey and Jack tiptoed out and went down to the bar, and Huey called for buttermilk for himself and Jack, and whatever the sheriff wanted. Abe said he'd take strawberry water with a little whisky in it, to celebrate the first time in history that Huey Haffener had stood treat for anything. To jump ahead, Lois got well, and she had almost nine hundred dollars saved up, and she took this and went up to Kimball County, Nebraska, and married a fella there, and made him a good wife. A happy ending to a sad story. He was a wheat farmer, but nobody can be all bad.

7

When they catched up with Rolf, he was back at his whittling, with his boot heels hooked in the bark of the rotten old log he was setting on, staring at the mud of the crick bank with his old hat on the back of his head. He gave them a look like he'd just as soon they'd let him alone. But Abe set down beside him, and Huey and Jack set down on the other side, and he seen he was cornered.

"Dr. Nobile is with her," Abe said. "He says she's going to be all right."

"He does, does he," Rolf said.

Huey said, "In fact, I never seen Lois look prettier, and I would of bet anything we was going to have to bury her stiff as a board."

"I never did think that, not after I talked to Bea," Abe said. "She might not know religion, but she knows whores, and I know enough about religion to feel sure of my ground. My grandmother was a Sephardic Spanish Jew, you know, and a lot of them Bible people was Jews."

"I never knowed that," Jack said.

"It's a fact! Ask Rolf," Abe said.

Jack asked him, and Rolf said why sure. He said, "In fact, our Lord Himself was a Jew, didn't you know that?"

"I may of heard it, but if I did, I forgot it," Abe said. "For all anybody knows, I may be descended from Him. I could have in my very own veins that Precious Blood they're always talking about."

Rolf said, "Abe, you're a fool! Our Lord died a single man, executed, you might say, as a felon. They railroaded Him, and they convicted Him on perjured testimony, and they executed Him fast so He couldn't take it up on appeal. Nobody on earth ever had a rawer deal than Him, and believe me, I'm a man who knows what it is to be unjustly convicted."

Abe said, "Well, I could still be related to Him. Over in Blessed Sacrament, they got a statue of Jesus that could pass for a Spaniard. I'll bet we both come down from the same line of people."

"Tell you what, Abe," Huey Haffener said. "Let's go down to the crick there, and you turn that water into wine, at least try your luck at it."

Rolf looked at him and said, "Mr. Haffener, I can't speak for a patient and forbearing God, but I'll tell you that from a personal point of view, you're being as offensive as a wet goat by a hot stove."

"Oh what are you so touchy about?" Huey said.

In former times, Rolf would of busted anybody that talked like that right in the nose, but he said, "Don't try my patience! I've had a hard time of it with that girl, and I saw the Lord heal her, and I'm in no mood for the kind of jokes you put out."

Huey twitched and grinned and batted his snot-colored eyes. He said, "Oh look here, you don't really mean the Lord come into that room and cured Lois, do you?"

Rolf said softly, "You don't believe that?"

Huey said, "Oh hell, of course not, do you think I was born yesterday?"

Rolf stood up off'n the log, and snapped his knife shut, and laid his whittling stick down, and put his hands on his hips. "Then you look me in the eye, Mr. Haffener," he said, "and tell me in plain short easy words what you see in me."

Huey said, "In you? Why a plain old cowboy, a nice enough fella, and you've got sand, nobody could of stood up to that old bitch that wanted Bea run out of the church without plenty of sand. Let's say, Ledger, I'd give even money on you to ride a bronc or skin a dead cow faster than anybody else. But on whomping up a miracle and summoning the Lord into a whorehouse, why you're on the short end of a million to one."

"So that's how you see it," Rolf said.

"Yes, and don't take offense. You asked me fair and square, and I told you fair and square," Huey said.

"I don't take offense. You got me pegged, I'd say. Now, you seen that woman in a rigid convulsion, didn't you?" Rolf said.

"No mistake about that, she was sure stiff," Huey admitted.

"You seen Dr. Nobile throw in his cards?" Rolf said.

"Yes, he's an honest man. If he can't help you, he says so, he don't just give you a sugar pill and send you a bill for a dollar," Huey admitted.

"You seen me go into that room with her, and you yourself helped lock me in there, didn't you?" Rolf said.

"We all seen that. What's your point?" Huey said.

"Well go see her now," Rolf said, "cleansed and well and happy, turned over a new leaf with her sins washed away. I was the only human bean in the room with her, and I couldn't heal a dog of the slobbers of my own power. Now if *I* didn't heal her, tell me this—*who did?*"

Huey just set there twitching and batting his eyes, and Abe said, "He's got you by the balls, Huey. Either Rolf did or God did, now one or the other."

Huey shook his head. "I'm only glad that it happened by daylight," he said. "It sure gives you the creeps, son of a bitch if it don't! The Lord Himself in that room, why I'll never be able to use it again."

Word of that healing spread over Mooney so fast you'd think there was a dozen wagon bridges over the crick and a brick road to each of them. They just deviled that poor cowboy to death. Everybody that had a hair crosswise, they wanted him to heal them. This one-legged man that worked in the livery barn, he wanted his leg back after thirty years.

There was some opposition. Frank Mueller, the butcher that had been the only witness to the escape of whoever killed Peg

Saymill, was a socialist. He wanted to know if Rolf could work a miracle, why didn't he raise the colonel from the dead? That was a good question, and Rolf admitted it.

He could only say that he wasn't a healer or a miracle worker, all he did was pray, and he'd done this plenty of times before, and never had no such crazy unexpected results. But he said he wasn't ashamed of it and he wouldn't back down on what happened, not if they lynched him. But he said he wasn't going to try it again, he felt too let down to work himself up like that, and they could like it or lump it.

There was one person wouldn't take no for an answer, Mrs. Mable McMurdoch, organist in the church, and wife of the banker. She pinned Rolf to a brick wall and leaned against the wall to shut him off on one side, and she shook her finger in his face to herd him back on the other.

She said, "Pastor, I know the power of prayer, and I know the limitations of those who pray, but I've got a little boy, a nephew I'm trying to raise, that I think falls within those finite limitations. You can help him. He got throwed from his pony a year ago September, and hurt his back. Dr. Nobile says it's healed long ago, but poor Emmet is afraid to try to walk, afraid of pain and failure, and I haven't the heart to make him because, God forgive me, I'm afraid too."

"So am I," Rolf said when he could pinch a word in by its thin edge.

"Well just roll up your sleeves and pretend you're not, Pastor," she said, "because I think you can get to this boy's cob, you might say, where nobody else could. No use asking my husband, he don't care much for Emmet anyway and he only puts up with prayer, but this is a case for a man."

"You expect too much of me," Rolf said.

"No I don't," she said. "I only expect you to try, but I have faith in you if not in myself, and I think you'll hearten that boy, and that's what he needs if he's going to take up his bed and walk. If he don't, Pastor, he's going to be a bedfast cripple all his life."

She catched Rolf by the arm, and dragged him home to

where she lived, and here was this kid, Emmet James Day, laying in a hammock under a tree, Day being her maiden name. Emmet was the son of her diseased brother. He was just laying there, looking up through the leaves. He was a puny little thing, and he didn't take no interest in Mrs. McMurdoch, and even less in Rolf.

A lot of people had follered them home to see the miracle, and they was tromping down Mable's flowers and taking turns getting a drink at the pump. Rolf told them to get out and give him elbow room with this spoiled little brat, and Mable made them get out of there. Rolf picked up a wooden box, and stood it on end beside the hammock, and he set down on it and started in.

Nobody seen or heard what happened, and Rolf never talked about it and neither did the kid, and the only sure thing was that the kid was right, it did hurt something awful, and he didn't pick up his bed and walk that day, not by any means. But he did get up on his feet, and he cried and cursed Rolf something awful, and Rolf got him back in his hammock and began showing him tricks with a deck of cards Emmet had. Rolf had always been good at card tricks, and in prison an old-timer had taught him a few that could of made him a rich man if he hadn't of swore off gambling. It wouldn't of been no gamble by then, though, the way he could deal a deck.

Later on that day, Mable heard the kid crying, and she went out in the back yard, and there he was up on his feet, trying to hobble from tree to tree, and saying, "Oh God it hurts, God-damn but it hurts, my son of a bitching back anyway." Mable cried, first because he was trying to walk, and second because he used that kind of language. But Rolf told her that every-body had his own way of praying, and first you got the kid up on his feet, and then you broke him of swearing. One thing at a time.

The next day he was going tree to tree, and then to the pump, and then to the woodshed, and before summer was over he had learned to spit between his teeth and skin the cat on a tree limb, and was a sore trial to that poor woman, he was so full of hell.

That's jumping ahead, but there was enough early signs for it to be another miracle, so before anybody else could make an offer, the Methodist board got together and voted to tie Rolf up. They would go as high as $2.50 a sermon, and fix the leak in the roof over the pulpit. They had a parsonage they could rent for eight dollars a month, so they was coming out of it dirt cheap. Although somebody said $2.50 for an hour's sermon is more than a single man has a right to expect, if he's holding down a steady job during the week, and can't visit the sick or comfort the dying between weekends.

Rolf must of said "no" a hundred times, as patient as possible, which wasn't very patient by nightfall, and he would of stuck to it except for one thing. This thing was Jack Butler, and Jack said, "Well if you ain't going to preach, what do you need with a fast horse to make a trip in every Sunday? You won't need Fanny then, will you? Pick out any other horse on the place for your working string, and let's put her back in the barn."

That was more than you could ask Rolf to stand, but he had this bullheaded streak in him, he quit saying "no" but he still wouldn't say "yes." So Abe got the board together quietly at Jimmy Drummond's office, and he got Rolf to go up there with him for some reason or other, and they broke the news that he was to be examined on faith and doctrine.

"That's what you think," Rolf said. "This job is over my head, and I know it, and you ain't going to examine me in faith and doctrine or anything else."

One of the board members said, "I don't know what it is you object to, Reverend; you believe in the Apostle's Creed, don't you?"

"More or less," Rolf said.

So they looked at each other, and then one of them said, "I believe we can pass this candidate for the Christian ministry with a thankful and joyous heart, and I so move." The others

said they would too, and they skinned him through the exam-
ination before Rolf knowed what was happening.

"Now you had better bless him with the laying on of hands,"
Jimmy Drummond said. "Reverend Ledger, you get down on
your knees, and let them form a circle around you."

"That I will never do," Rolf said.

"I see," Jimmy said, "you're a proud old cowboy that can
work miracles, a lot of gall anybody has got to expect you to
kneel before the Lord."

"Somebody is going to pay for this," Rolf said. He knelt
down, and they all put their hands on him, and Jimmy Drummond told somebody to pray that their candidate be accepta-
ble unto God, that being a form he had found successful in
Principles of Ecclesiastical Law. So old McMurdoch, he said,
"Lord, we bring Thee a preacher to preach Thy word, and
before Thou findest fault with him, consider our need. We
ain't much of a congregation, and the longer this pulpit stands
empty, the worse it will be. Look with pity on us, Lord, hung
up on this side of the Continental Divide, neither frontier nor
farm nor good honest cow country, drifters passing through
like the dispossessed Children of Israel, and half of them don't
have no idee where they're going. Thy beaver is gone from
Thy streams, Thy buffalo has vanished, and Thy Indians with
them, and when we look at some of the riffraff that has took
their place, we see we have only went from bad to worse, because there's nothing worse than a bad white man, as Thou
knowest. Oh Lord, we need preaching and guidance, and a
strong hand on a severe bit, or here goes another of Thy
churches the way of the beaver and the buffalo. If our candidate for Thy ministry don't look like suchamuch, look at what's
left to pick from, and who's doing the picking. Make the best
of what we have, oh Lord, and help him as Thee did across the
crick, because we need it as bad as that woman, amen."

Somebody helped Rolf stand up, and Abe took off his neck-
erchief and wiped his eyes. "I may hear worse prayers than
that before I die, Mac," he said, "but I'll never hear a better."

"A man does the best he can," McMurdoch said.

Jimmy Drummond drawed up an affidavit for them to sign, saying they had examined Rolf in faith and doctrine, and found him sound in wind and limb. It stated that the examiners knowed of their own knowledge of a healing caused by the candidate's prayers for a contrite sinner he had brought to penitence, and that the congregation was all good Methodists, and that they hadn't heard nothing repugnant in his preaching to the good old Methodist creed, and that his unjust term in prison had taught the candidate how firm a foundation his life rested on, and so forth. They all signed it, and Jimmy swore them in as a notary public.

"This'll go to Denver by the U.S. Mail," Jimmy said, "but the gossip about healing that poor woman will beat it there. The bishop will either take you up on it, or there'll be a stampede of the other denominations in here, with more ordinations than you'll know what to do with."

"I still ain't going to preach steady in that church and I don't consider myself an ordained minister," Rolf said. "I don't mind helping the church out in a pinch, but enough is enough."

"That's up to you," Jimmy said. "You remember, though, that the church property follows the pulpit, and any time there's real estate at stake, ecclesiastical law is no different than the civil law—it'll find a good sound loophole to secure title. You may not feel ordained, but you'll get the patent or whatever they call it in the mail, and you take notice, it'll be dated today."

They thought they had themselves a minister, but they didn't know that old cowboy. He made up his mind right then that he would stay long enough to buy himself some new pants and a shirt, and maybe a suit of underwear, and if he could stand it that long, a new hat. And then he was going to light out some night, and change his name if he had to, because this was just more responsibility than he wanted to take on. Swearing off a few things is all right, most people backslide on them resolutions sooner or later, and Rolf looked on his oaths as a way of sliding back into civilian life a little at a time. But they wasn't fooling *him*, ordination was worse than getting married for tying a man down, and he meant to be long gone and unheard from before that bishop replied.

The truth was, Rolf was rattled bad by what had happened to that girl and that little boy. He never had backed down on a job or a dare, no sir, especially if there was one chance in a million it would work, and he went into both of them deals in that spirit, what did he have to lose but a little time? He had seen prayer fall flat as a pancake many a time, like every summer in Smith County, Kansas, when people a lot more righteous than him never let up petitioning the Lord for rain, and it never did rain, and a few times people prayed not to let somebody die, and they went ahead and died anyway. It just beat the thunder to him, how his prayers had worked on that poor miserable whore and that little boy.

He kept trying to get out of town to think it over, so's he'd have a ready answer for people that pestered him, but they kept coming up wanting to shake hands, or just to touch him, especially women, and what they wanted to do was grab and not just touch. A lot of people brought babies for him to bless.

He told them, "I can't bless nobody. I can only ask the Lord to do that, and you can do that much yourself." But you know how well that went over; no, they just wouldn't let him alone until he had put his hand on that baby's head, and shut his eyes and said a quick little short prayer, and then if he couldn't get out of it, kissed the baby. People are that kind of fools about their kids. Even if they don't take much stock in religion most of the time, they won't take a chance on their kids missing out on something.

There was going to be a full moon, but it was all clouded over, and was darker than a yard down a cow's throat before he busted away from people. He didn't know that town at all, and he walked into a couple of fences and one clothesline, and he started some dogs to baying, and he finally found himself blundering around down on the bank of the crick. He tripped over something and fell down on his knees, and he reckoned that as long as he was there, he might as well try a prayer or two for himself, and see if it done him half as much good as it did that girl and that little boy.

Well, finely he had to get up without no answer whatever, not one indication that the Lord was taking in any filings that day, court was closed as far as Rolf could tell. He was getting hungry anyway, so he pointed toward the lamps and pretty soon got back into town, not any more of a mess than you might think except for the knees of his pants, where he had went down in the mud. And the first people he seen was the Venaman family, in town to buy their month's groceries at the stores. Cal had already heard the news, and he wanted to shake Rolf's hand, and he seemed to be amused anyway at the news.

"You have unique qualifications and a unique opportunity, Parson," he said. "I'd like to have your own story of that girl's miraculous healing sometime."

"I ain't going to talk about it," Rolf said.

"Well, I'll respect your reticence. I hear it even gave Huey Haffener a jolt," Cal said.

"Well, he stopped twitching for a minute, and when he does, he just looks flabby all over," Rolf said.

"You've got Huey sized up. We'll see you day after tomorrow. Like everyone else, we'll make a special effort to get to church," Cal said.

"Day after tomorrow? Me and Jack thought this was Saturday!" Rolf said.

"No, it's only Friday. Don't feel badly about losing track of only a day. Living with Jack Butler, I can see how you'd lose a week easily," Cal said.

Rolf shook hands with Cal again, and then with Opal, and then with Winnie, and when he turned to shake with Samantha, she just deliberately didn't put her hand out to shake. She looked down at the muddy knees of his pants instead.

"I see you didn't lose any time putting on the public badge of your trade, Reverend," she said.

Rolf said, "I was just walking in the dark, ma'am, and I plainly and simply fell, that's all."

"I see!" Samantha said. "I'd clean those pants if I were you, Reverend. You're liable to mislead people into thinking you had been praying."

"They'd be right, ma'am, if they thought that. As long as I was down there, I thought I might as well."

"Oh?" she said. "If it isn't too personal, what does a new minister pray for immediately after the rite of ordination, or whatever it was?"

Rolf said, "Humility, Miss Samantha. I never was any too well stocked with it, and it seems to be in mighty short supply in sections of this congregation, too."

Cal laughed, but nobody else did, although Opal and Winnie swallered a little air, and got a little purple in the face, and couldn't look at each other. Rolf just walked off and left them, wondering what in tarnation had made him say a thing like that, because he never in his life had so much as used that word before, only read it, yet "humility" sprung to his mind as quick as a mouse trap snapping. And he knowed that words could be a vice too, yes they could, and he'd have to watch that in the future.

8

He found Jack pretty soon after that, blessedly sober as a judge, but spiritually buoyed up by what had happened to Lois until he just talked Rolf's leg off on the way home. He had some of the peculiarest idees about religion, like they was going to have a regular parade of women coming out there to the J Bar B to own up to their sins, and he said he didn't want a lot of fallen women giving the J Bar B a bad name, but what was really ailing him was that he had women on the brain. But Rolf let the talk roll off like water on a duck's back, and before the week was out, Jack had to face up to it that life was just stringing fence, nothing more.

They knocked off early Saturday morning, when Jack said he wanted to go into town and buy some bolts and washers and stuff. Rolf said, "Are you sure you don't want to liquor up, now? You don't have to lie to me."

"I never was in better shape to stand off my demon," Jack said. "All I want is some half-inch carriage bolts and washers."

They got an early enough start, but then they found one of Cal Venaman's horses bogged down in the mud, and they had to stop and pull it out, and then go back to the J Bar B and change clothes, so it was suppertime before they got to Mooney. Jack went over to the Jackrabbit where he always stayed, and Rolf was going to blow four bits on a room over the livery barn, only he run into Marcus Sippy and nothing would do but what he'd come there. It was his first experience with how women will flourish their cooking at the preacher, and trot out fruit jars their families didn't know they had, when their own husband was lucky to get bread and bacon-grease gravy for supper. Rolf went with Marcus, who sold harness and saddles, and his wife Blanche taught a Sunday school class and made missionary didies out of flour sacks. Everybody called her Blanche, whether they knowed her well or not, because you try saying "Mrs. Sippy" over and see what comes out.

Their supper was over and the kids was in bed, but Blanche took out the back door on a dead run when she seen Rolf coming with Marcus, and Rolf heard one strangled squawk and then another, and then a lot of flopping in the dried weeds, and he knowed two big fryers had been sacrificed in his honor. Marcus set Rolf down in the parlor, and give him the album to look at, and then he excused himself and went out.

Pretty soon he come back and set down too. Marcus had soldiered in the cavalry, and been in the Black Hills like Rolf, but somehow they couldn't get a conversation going, and Rolf knowed why. Marcus had excused himself to have a little snort, and then that wasn't enough, after he set down again he slipped off his boots, and there was a hole in one sock that let his big toe stick out, and he didn't know whether to put his boots back on or just pretend nothing had happened.

Then one of the kids hollered he had wet the bed, and all they could do was set there and rock and try to talk about the weather. But it had been clear and warm and dry for so long, with summer coming on, that finely they was both saying things like yes that's true, it certainly was a good open spring this year, that's right. Rolf knowed he had to take the bull by the horns or they was never going to stop pulling against each other.

He said, "Mr. Sippy, I hope the fact that I'm temporarily your minister don't make you uncomfortable in your own home. There couldn't be nobody commoner than me."

"What mortifies me," Marcus said, "is that Jacob wet the bed, and he's the one you're going to sleep with. He ain't done that in a long time."

"Don't worry, I don't mind a bit," Rolf said, and it was his first white lie as a preacher, and he reckoned it prob'ly wouldn't be his last.

Pretty soon Blanche said, "Five minutes! I set three places, Papa, because I know you'll want to eat and I do too; my, we'll be both as fat as Watertown geese, but land sakes how often do we get to enjoy a meal without the kids?"

Rolf and Marcus washed up, and then Marcus excused himself again, and had another little nip to steady to his hospitality chores, and he steadied too hard. He got to preening on Blanche's cooking, and how she could raise a chicken to be four or five pounds without getting too tough to fry, and so on.

"It sure is delicious," Rolf said. "I never et better fried chicken in my life, and there's nothing I love more than milk gravy from chicken grease."

"Blanche is part Scotch-Irish and part German," Marcus said. "You can't beat that combination."

He talked so much that he got Blanche nervous, and the way she kept watching him made Rolf nervous, and Marcus knowed it. He was one of these men who like to have a thing out in the open, even if it does embarrass you, so finally he blurted it out.

He said, "Reverend, I take a little nip every night before supper, but to my shame and sorrow, tonight I took a second one because I'm a poor host without something to touch off my kindling. That's a mighty poor excuse for imitating Jack Butler, but it's all I got."

Blanche just glared at him, but Rolf said, "I don't know why you feel you have to confess to me. I'm white-ribbon myself now, all the way, but in my time I have downed my share of the rotgut, and I figger it this way. So long as you carry it like a gentleman, and don't have to charge it at the saloon, and don't bring shame on your family or pass out like Jack Butler, what you do is your own affair."

"Reverend, Methodists is temperance!" Blanche said.

"I know that," Rolf said, "and it's their own affair, but you just show me where it mentions temperance in the Ten Commandments, ma'am."

Marcus said, "There, ain't that what I always said? Temperance means being temperate, and I'm a temperate drinker. Did you ever see me stewed?"

Blanche began to leak tears, and she said, "I have to say that's the truth, Reverend, it's not a problem for Papa, but we get the church papers and they're *so* down on liquor! A body don't know what to think."

"I know what I think," Rolf said. "Drunkenness is a sin, like sloth and lust and usury and lying, and I'll pray over a sot as long as anybody will hold him down, or until he's redeemed. But if we keep out everybody that takes a nip for his nerves, or a cold now and then, we shut the door on some of our best Christians."

She busted out weeping and said, "Have some more chicken, have some more fried potatoes, have some more creamed baby turnips."

Rolf was beginning to see he had to watch himself, because he had a gift of loosening people up he'd never suspicioned before. Until he went to prison, he had more of a tightening gift. He could go into a perfectly calm store or saloon or auction barn, and look the material over, and pick his man, and in two minutes all you'd see was elbows and feet, and all you'd hear was grunts and people yelling not to upset the stove. Them good old days was gone forever, but he meant to do the best he could as long as he was on this job, with no regrets. Just watch himself that he didn't loosen people into loading him down with a lot of nasty personal problems he couldn't help with.

Word had got around considerable, that Rolf was a good sound preacher, and single, and everybody with unmarried daughters anywhere from thirteen to fifty was there, and no Abe Whipple to help herd them. They said Abe had went out to see about some kind of a robbery, and the board wasn't no help, in fact it looked to Rolf that most of them favored somebody's daughter, usually one that needed all the help she could get.

He preached to a mighty good crowd, taking as his text Romans 11:1, I say then, Hath God cast away His people? God forbid. You can make just about anything you want out of that, so it's a mighty safe text for a new preacher, and when Rolf went into the pulpit instead of the lectern for the first time, he needed something good and safe. It just scared the dickens out of him, that pulpit. He said the difference was, when you spoke from the lectern, you was just any old body reading the Bible or something else, anybody could do that, some claimed even women, although that was going pretty far. But when you went into that pulpit, you was delivering a message from God, or at least *for* Him, and it was like the difference between transubstantiation and consubstantiation, it might be only a word, but so was hell only a word in a way. It depended not just on *what* you said, but *where* you said it and *how* you said it and *why*. Even if you talked like a fool,

if it was from the pulpit, some fool was going to take it for the
Gospel.

But he skinned through all right, claiming that they might
feel cast away out there in Colorado, but the opposite was
true; if they had that feeling it was because *they* had cast away
God. He paid his respects to them that had struggled to hold
the church together, although not at any great expense to
anybody, and he said if they thought they had problems, they
should of read up on them Romans that Paul was writing to.
He said they was some of the most miserable people he ever
heard of, with a perfect right to think they had been cast away.
They had to hide down in the tunnels where they buried their
dead, because it was against the law to be a Christian in them
days, and they was all on the dodge.

And so on. They took up a collection, with Marcus Sippy
and Alf Constable, the ushers, taking it up, with everybody
keeping a mighty sharp eye on them. Then they sung another
hymn or two, and Rolf asked Alf to lead them in prayer, because he looked like a man who could do it, and he could.
They had another song, and then Rolf prayed and give the
benediction, and then Mable McMurdoch pinned the people
down with some music until he could get outside to shake
hands as they marched out.

It was like slipping into any other job; you done the best you
could and copied the workmen you admired the most, and
that was all anybody could do. He shook hands with everybody, and they all told him how much they was inspired by
his sermon, and he thanked them one and all. When Liz Saymill shook hands, she slipped a ten-dollar bill into his hand
and whispered, "I hope you never lose your refreshing inno-
cence, Reverend," and so he could really thank her with deep
feeling.

He told Alf Constable he'd be proud to have Sunday noon
dinner with him, because he didn't see no way out of it, Alf
was just busting with pride over being picked to lead in prayer,
but Rolf said he had to look up Jack Butler first, to make sure
he wasn't yielding to his demon. Nobody could really follow

him across the crick to make sure that was all he was going to do, but they made sure they hung around that part of town to see how long it took him.

He was just starting down the bank of the crick when this Irishman come across the footlog. His name was Bill Ahern, and he owned a half-interest in an eight-horse freight outfit that was making a little money, and he had been married to a local girl until she died suddenly. A well woman one day, and three months later dead of a terrible eating tumor in her female organs. Bill claimed to of fought fifty-eight rounds with the champion of Wales, and knocked him out.

Bill got to be a problem when his wife died, getting drunk every time he got lonesome, which was every time he got in from a freight trip, and then going out and looking for somebody worth whipping. Most of them wasn't, but he whipped them anyway. It took five or six men to arrest him, and volunteers had got scarce, so mostly Abe Whipple tried to reason with him. Sometimes he could and sometimes he couldn't and today he was out of town on this robbery.

Bill had quite a brogue, especially drunk, so you could tell by it how much he had drunk. He had on hobnailed teamster boots and was carrying his shirt over his shoulder. He always took his shirt off when he was looking for somebody worth whipping, so he wouldn't have to stop and take it off then, and risk a chance the fella would get away.

Rolf didn't have no idee who Bill Ahern was, only that he was a big drunk with no shirt on, on a Sunday, but he stepped aside and said, "Good morning." Bill stopped and looked at him, and he seen there wasn't no fair fight in anybody Rolf's size, and all it done was annoy him to be spoke to when his mind was on a fight.

He said, "Well, Jesus Christ, what difference does it make what kind of a morning it is? I'm tired of that kind of talk. You can't do nothing about what kind of a day it is."

His brogue was so thick it was hard to understand him, but Rolf did, and he said, "Well, what we can't help, we can either endure or enjoy, I reckon."

"Jesus Christ, are you saying you're going to *make* me enjoy it?" Bill said. "Even if I don't feel like it?"

Rolf said, "No, my friend, and this is twice you've used the name of the Lord in vain to me. I'm a sort of a deputy minister of the gospel, and I resent it, and you don't hurt me, only your own immortal soul and what manliness you have, if you have any. Just a reminder."

"You're a piss-poor specimen," Bill said.

"I know when somebody's twisting my tail to make me beller," Rolf said, "and I ain't going to beller. But I'm purely tired of standing here arguing, and I ask you man to man to let me pass."

Bill swang at him, and Rolf seen it coming and rolled backwards uphill, staying out of the mud, and coming up on his feet again hardly spitting any blood at all. You could hear Bill all over town, and most of the men from the church suddenly passed up propriety in favor of not missing anything, and if you'd passed the hat up there on top of the bank, you'd of had the cream of society to deal with.

Not that anybody made any move when they seen Bill knock the new preacher down. There was enough of them to swarm over him like bees, and weight him down several deep, but a thing like that takes leadership, and leadership don't necessarily pop out when it's most needed. Rolf felt his way back uphill backward when he come to his feet, and he dusted his clothes off a little and said:

"You hit like a man who knows how to fight, then you ought to have sense enough to know you didn't land that one. Well, then you ought to have sense enough to know I can whip you if I have to."

Them people up on the bank just purely panted at that, not a gasp but a whole gale of panting, like they was thinking has this young preacher gone crazy or what? Talking about whipping Bill Ahern.

Bill said, "You can what? Jesus Christ, you couldn't lick the cream crock with the cat."

"That does it," Rolf said.

He come down the path, and Bill smiled and throwed away his shirt, and doubled up his fists, and he had fists the size of the hoof of a Shire horse, and about as hard, and arms like cottonwood limbs. Well he come at Rolf swinging, and then there he was sliding back down towards the crick on his hind end, blood puddling out of his nose and one eye closing up.

He said, "Say that was some trick, let's see you do it again." He stood up and licked his thumb, and people knowed that when Bill licked his thumb, watch out because he was getting ready to enjoy himself.

Rolf said, "My friend, I learned to fight in prison. You're prob'ly fairly tough, but where your kind of fighting leaves off, that's where prison fighting begins."

So Bill jumped him again, and come down on nothing, and then Rolf was all over him, hitting him with his fists whenever he seen his chance, but also with knees and elbows and boot heels, and the top of his head. Every time Bill got up, Rolf knocked him down, until finely he did let Bill get up and catch hold of the bushes to stay up. He asked Bill if he had enough, and Bill said no he was just getting started.

He come in for more, and this time he really got it, and there wasn't no way Rolf could quit, because as long as Bill could move, even his little finger, or one toe, he was ready to fight. Finely he couldn't even move them, and a couple of men had to come down from the top of the bank and help Rolf carry him up.

"He is just a troublemaker," Rolf said. "Anybody that fights on Sunday only wants to make trouble."

"That's right in a way," somebody said, "but Bill used to be harmless except on payday, but since he lost his wife he has been pure poison."

"Well why did he have to take it out on me?" Rolf said.

"He had already took it out on everybody else, Reverend," this fella said.

"That's a mighty poor excuse," Rolf said, "but leave me alone with him. I never lost anybody near and dear to me, but it must be pretty bad," Rolf told him.

"She was sure dear to him," this fella said. "He just doted on that girl."

Bill come to, and him and Rolf was alone except for two or three dozen people that had stepped back to a decent distance. Bill said, "Give me a few minutes, and I'm your man again. You're a good dirty fighter, my kind."

Rolf said, "I found out why you want to fight everybody, because you lost your wife."

Bill said, "Drop that you slobber-mouth pious son of a bitch, you're not fit to mention her name."

Rolf said, "I don't even know her name, I only say my heart goes out to you, and I forgive you wanting to fight me, because that kind of suffering comes only from love, and God has nothing but mercy for a heart full of love, and who am I to argue with Him? But I'll tell you this much, Bill, that wife of yours is now with Him, and my hunch is she feels this foolishness has to come to an end, she prob'ly didn't like your fighting when she was alive, and it don't seem logical she'd be for it now."

"I *wish* you'd shut *up* about her, how *much* can a man *stand?*" Bill said.

Rolf said, "As much as he has to. The Lord giveth and the Lord taketh away, blessed be the name of the Lord. You can't fight this with your fists, or with the hardness of your heart if you've got any. Only grace can help you, and don't ask me what grace is because I can't tell you, only that if you had it you wouldn't go around shaming your wife's memory the way you do. And you look me in the eye and tell me this, Bill—besides being a sin and a public disgrace, what good does it do you?"

"Nothing, but I can't stand it if I don't," Bill said. "She was the best woman! You just get your hands on something good in life, and it slips away from you. The only thing really good in my life was that woman."

Rolf said, "I ain't got no answer to you. I never had your experience, and anyways I'm only a man, and not suchamuch of a one at that. Who you need to grab hold of the other side of this heavy pail handle is God. You've tried everything else,

Bill. If you want, I'll be glad to lead these neighbors of yours in a little prayer. What have you got to lose?"

"Nothing I reckon," Bill said.

So they all bowed their heads, and them that had hats on took them off, and Rolf opened by reminding the Lord that He was responsible for this man's mess by taking his wife, and it was up to Him to ante up now. He said it surely wasn't no offhand whim of the Lord's to take her, but part of a plan, and he wasn't trying to tell Him how to run His business, but he did feel some responsibility for this poor bereaved trouble-making Bill Ahern. He said it wasn't going to be no easy job to touch Bill's heart with grace, but it couldn't be much harder than turning water into wine, like he done at the wedding in Cana. He wound up with an over-all general apology for the worthlessness of people in general and Bill in particular, and then he said, "Let Bill know some way, and You can do it if You put Your mind to it, that Bill's wife is still doing the best she can to take care of him, only he won't let her, this we ask in Christ's name, amen."

Bill was still setting down, and at this he covered his face with his hands and let out a yell. "I can see her face in my mind! I see her, I see her, I had forgot her dear face, but now I see her again!"

"That's grace, Bill," Rolf said.

Bill started blubbering around, and pounding the dirt with his fist, and he said, "I forgot what her face looked like. That was what hurt. You just have no idee how it hurt! She wasn't a pretty woman, you ask anybody though and they'll tell you that Grace was a good woman, really good, and now somehow it's like I partly got her back."

"Was her name Grace?" Rolf said.

"Why sure, what did you think?" Bill said.

Rolf said, "Well all right, just cut out this trying to whip everybody. I don't care how good you are, you're going to run into somebody that can whip you."

"You for instance?" Bill said. "We'll try that again sometime, when I'm sober."

"Not me," Rolf said. "God. Nobody can whip Him."

9

A healing is all right, there's prime material for popularity in it, but for downright public idolatry, nothing equals winning a good fight over a man nobody thought nobody could whip. Even Huey Haffener come out of his prairie-dog hole to shake Rolf's hand, and Rolf said it was like handling a piece of hog liver.

"I only regret I missed the spectacle," Huey said. "I'm a great admirer of the manly art."

"I'm sorry it happened," Rolf said, "and I'm sure Bill wasn't at his best, was at his worst in fact."

"It's when Bill is at his worst that you want to worry, padre. Tell you what I'm going to do, I'm going to make a donation to your church."

Rolf said, "Well that will be appreciated, Huey, the Lord don't take no account of where money comes from, but you might examine your spirit in giving it." Huey took out his purse, and fished around in it quite a while, and made up a dollar out of quarters, dimes, and a nickel, and on second thought added another quarter to it, making $1.25.

Rolf said, "Are you sure you can afford this, Huey? I don't want your impulsiveness to run you short of the necessities of life."

You couldn't get Huey's goat any way about money, but he did scowl and scrounge around and come up with another $1.25 in silver, making $2.50 in all.

Rolf said, "Tell you what I'd ruther do, Huey. You take this back, and I'll go down there and take up a collection among your girls, and you match it."

Huey said, "You're a hell of a bargainer for a man of the cloth," and he handed Rolf a $10 gold piece, and got out before Rolf could twirl his rope for a foot catch. Making $12.50 in all, a record for Huey. Bill Ahern had turned Huey's place upside down more than once, and Huey himself once, and sloshed his head on the floor and into his spittoons, and it should of been worth $100 to Huey. But try getting it out of him.

A man likes to be liked, but Rolf had learned to make do with what human kindness leaked through the bars of a prison, which is just about none, and this overflow of appreciation had him edgy, so the harness was beginning to gald. Also he couldn't find Jack Butler, and he feared the worst.

So it was a relief to get free of people and go home with Alf Constable to dinner, which was roast pork loin with fresh spring greens and canned gooseberry sauce from last year's crop, and cinnamon rolls with raisins in them, and then green-apple cobbler from this year's crop. Alf run a feed and seed store, and also handled some horse medicine, and he raised garlic, and also fed about two hundred hogs a year. This was a nice two-hundred-and-fifty-pound barrow that accidentally got himself kicked in the head the night before, but Alf stuck it less than a minute after it happened, and an old-time butchering man like him, it didn't take him no time at all to boil up water to scald it in. A real good loin of roast fresh pork. One year, Alf shipped more than one hundred and forty pounds of garlic to Denver, where there was a lot of foreigners working around there in the mines who would eat it. His wife, Keziah, wouldn't have it in the house. Keziah was a Travis and originally a Presbyterian, but she made the switch to Methodist without any strain.

After they had finished eating, and Keziah went out to give the scraps to the dogs, Alf said, "Reverend, you look pretty peaked to me. Are people pestering the dickens out of you? It looks like that to me."

Rolf said, Well, he couldn't complain of the kindness they intended, but it was beginning to raise his sweat. So Alf said, "All right, you come with me, I'll show you the best little old hide-out in town. Nobody else knows about it, but you feel free to sneak in here and use it any time these people bear down on you too hard."

He showed Rolf a hammock he had slung between two trees out beside his hogpen, under some Concord grape vines that was just setting on green grapes. He said, "Reverend, do you know what, I killed a man once." Rolf said no, he hadn't heard that, and Alf said, "Well, I did. I didn't go to, it was over a woman, and the shame is, it was after I was married to Keziah. I was fooling around with her, and it's no excuse that she was a loose woman and easy to fool around with, a man makes that decision himself. Well there was another fella fooling around there too, and to make a long story short, him and me came to blows, and I knocked him pizzle-end upwards, and he come at me with a knife. Now I don't know what was in *his* mind, but I know that in *my* mind, all I wanted to do was knock that knife out of his hand and get out of there once and for all. Well what happened, I hit him with a chair and knocked him down, and he fell on his own knife and cut his own throat."

"That's a sad story," Rolf said.

"Yes it is. You can't give life back. Well this woman said for me to light a shuck out of town, this poor misguided dead bastard had often enough threatened to hang himself over her, and it wouldn't be no problem making people believe he'd cut his throat instead. This was down in Waxahachie, Texas. I was down there looking for some likely feeder steers for a fella on commission, and I was on the first train out of there you can really believe, headed back to St. Louis where me and Keziah was living. She don't know about this to this day. I never told it to anybody but you."

"I don't know what to say," Rolf said. "It ain't my place to say you're forgiven, although I'm sure in my heart that you are. Most forgiveness, if you ask me, comes from a heart that's heartily sorry."

"I hope I am," Alf said. "I'll tell you this much, Reverend, when that thing troubles me, or anything else troubles me, I just lay here and look up through them grape leaves to the sky, and prayer seems to mean more here than it does even in the church. I hope you won't take offense at that. It's a kind of a pagan way of looking at things, but that's how it is."

Rolf said he could sure enough understand it, he'd laid in a prison cell too many miserable days and nights not to appreciate being outdoors, and he was the last man in the world to say God wouldn't come close to a hogpen. Alf said, "Well, Reverend, you ain't old and you ain't learned, but you talk straight from the shoulder and you whipped Bill Ahern, and you may have more of a power in you than you suspicion. I'm glad I told you. I do feel better—maybe not entirely forgiven, but like I was getting there."

Alf went back to the house, and Rolf laid down in that hammock and thought, My goodness, what a lot of unhappiness people got themselves into, and then dumped it all on the minister, and all he could do was try to keep his knees from buckling and take it. He said to himself, Well I ain't up to it, that's for sure; imagine me trying to give comfort or guidance to a man like Alf Constable, why he ought to be guiding me, ruther.

He stretched out, and loosened his feet in his boots, and it felt mighty good. He could look up through them grape leaves that twined back and forth between them two trees, and there was a nice fresh breeze blowing, toward the hogpen instead of from it, and it blowed the grape leaves and the hammock too. Every now and then the hammock ropes would creak, and every now and then he'd see a twinkle of blue sky up there through the leaves, or maybe the white of summer clouds, and you can just guess what happened. He got two and a half hours of the best sleep he ever got in his life.

When he woke up, his first thought was that he hadn't been so rested since he went to prison, he could go out there and rope cows from hell to breakfast tomorrow, or do the branding and cutting if he was told, and go until dark. For a minute there he was carefree as a jaybird, a plain old no-account cowboy with not a worry in the world except where his next meal was coming from.

And then it come over him, the job he had took on, and he whipped both of his hands over his eyes, he felt so bad all of a sudden. He had never had the least desire to be a preacher, even temporary, and had agreed to be assistant chaplain only to get out of that clammy cistern. He said out loud, "No sir, I can't do it, it's too much, it's just ridiculous that's what, and I'd only fail so why ruin my own life and everybody else's too?"

He never knowed a preacher that enjoyed life, and their families was usually peaked-looking and timid, dressed in hand-me-downs, and cutting each other's hair. Their wives had to be nice to every woman in town, and when you consider the women the best Christians marry, there's no heavier curse on Adam's daughters. If a woman said to the preacher's wife, "That's a beautiful dress you got on, I don't see how you do it, I know I can't afford anything like it, I surely do admire how you manage," what she really meant was, "I know how much your husband makes, not much and it's still more than he's worth, and either somebody give you that or something funny is going on, and in either case, you ought to keep your place and not try to be fancier than the people that support you."

When a preacher's son got into a fight, he was a renegade bully, and when he didn't, he was a coward. He had to go to prayer meeting as well as church, and set there and look at the other boys, and wonder whose hand-me-down clothes he'd get next, so it was a wonder they didn't all turn out to be train robbers. When a preacher had daughters it was even worse, and if they was pretty, he was better off hit by a cyclone. If they played post office like the other girls at Halloween parties, on October 31, you bet on November 1 it was all over town how wanton they was, and if they didn't play, you wondered who they was kissing on the sly. If they married well, people said they had to, they'd been caught doing it, and if they married badly, people said what did you expect, girls like them.

If a preacher went into the barbershop, you can bet it wasn't for a haircut, it was to ask for a free calendar or to borrow his extra scissors because his wife had broke hers and he couldn't afford new ones. When he went in, everybody stopped talking, and some fella would say, "Well, Reverend, I was in the middle of a story, it's a little raw, but I reckon you like to let out the curb of your bit now and then, so I'll go right ahead." If the preacher walked out, why he was a hypocritical old son of a bitch all over town, and if he stayed, why *that* was all over town too, that the pious old son of a bitch had a dirty mind.

Rolf had had no use for preachers as a boy, and laying there in that hammock, he suddenly remembered why. When he was about ten years old back in Smith County, or maybe eleven, there was an old retired preacher, Reverend Hood, who come around every second Sunday with his wife, for chicken and dumplings with the Ledgers. They drove a gray mare so old she had gone first white and then sort of yellowish, by the name of Birdie, that they had raised from a colt. They had a creaky old top-buggy Reverend Hood kept shined up like a new saloon, it being the only way he had to pass the time. The other preachers in town wouldn't cut him in on calling on the sick, the aged, and the bereaved, because they said the next thing they knowed, he'd be cutting himself in on weddings and funerals too, and there went all semblance of regularity, and without regularity where was Christianity?

Reverend Hood wore an old derby hat, and a celluloid collar, and a ratty old black silk tie, and he was so nearsighted that if Birdie hadn't of knowed the roads, he just never would have got anywhere. His wife was about as ugly as a woman can be, so maybe it was just as well his eyesight was bad. She was always sewing, setting there in her buggy stitching away, with a black lace cap on her head, and her thimble on, and it was that thimble that was Rolf's mess of pottage as the saying is.

When old Birdie slouched into the yard, dragging the Hoods in that old wobble-wheel buggy, Rolf and his older brother Eddie was supposed to lope down and take care of the horse. They also had to help them out of the buggy, the

Reverend first and then Mrs. Hood, and Eddie wouldn't do it because he said they smelled bad. So it was always Rolf had to.

Reverend Hood would pat Rolf on the head and say, "Take care of the mare, lad, she has served me loyally for many a year, give her a measure of oats, that's a good lad," and you could bet if she ever got any oats they was mooched at the same time the Hoods was mooching their chicken and dumplings. Then when Rolf went around to help Mrs. Hood out, she said, "Give me your hand, boy, look lively now!" She come down on him like the smokehouse caving in, and then she had to huff and grunt and belch getting turned around and aimed towards the house. All this time her weight was on Rolf, and she wasn't no small woman, no, not by any means. Then just when she was aimed right, and ready to be fired, before he could duck loose from her, she'd rap him over the head with that thimble.

He thought he could have stood anything else, the long prayers that Reverend Hood spooled off before dinner, and the Hoods getting the best parts of the chicken, and the biggest slabs of pie—they was welcome to that for all of Rolf, but *why* did she have to whack him on the head with that thimble?

One hot Sunday in August, old Birdie come slouching up the lane, and Rolf knowed he should of expected it because his mother had killed a hen, but he had been living in a fool's paradise as a boy will. He had a new horse in fact, and while he hadn't rode him yet, and could barely lead him around, he was laying there in the shade dreaming of when he'd be old enough to be a train robber on that very horse.

It wasn't really a horse, just a little spotted Shetland pony stud that Rolf's father had picked up in a swap. Three years old, not much higher than hip-high to a tall Indian as the saying goes, and so mean and spoiled it took a good man to handle him.

This pony stud, Trinket, was carrying on something fierce from his lot behind the barn. Rolf helped Reverend Hood out of the buggy, and then he helped Mrs. Hood out, and she whacked him over the head with her thimble, and they went creepy-crawling up towards the house the way real, real old folks will. Rolf and his brother Eddie unhooked the mare Birdie, and was going to put her in the barn and give her a bait of oats, as per usual.

But the old mare was cutting up real frisky, whipping her tail and stomping her feet, and finally she let out a blast at the pony, poor old undefiled preacher's mare that she was.

Rolf said, "Eddie, you know what? This Goddamn old mare is horsing, that's what?" Eddie said that couldn't be, she must be twenty years old, too old for that stuff, and Rolf said, "Well just look at her. Eddie, I feel sorry for this old mare! Listen, take her into the barn and peel off the harness, but leave her bridle on. I'll put a bridle on Trinket, and when I holler, you bring her out back of the barn to the tank."

Eddie was the oldest, and if he had ever had a dishonorable thought in his life he suppressed it well, and this just shocked the hell out of him. But even if he was the oldest, Rolf was the boss buck there, and Eddie was prob'ly just as curious as Rolf to see if that religious old mare was capable of it.

The barn was built on a sidehill, with the horse barn on the high side, and the cowbarn on the low side. There was a tank from the windmill set in a fence, to water both cows and horses, and on the low side, so the cows could get to it, Rolf's father had built a platform of dirt, held in by a brick wall about two feet high, with a ramp up both sides of it.

This is where they tried it out, the mare on the low side with her hind end up against the brick wall, and Trinket on the platform. It was the first time Rolf ever tried to handle that pony alone, but Trinket had only one thing on his mind, and he got onto it mighty quick, what they expected of him.

To make a long story short, if horses enjoy it as much as they look, Birdie paid off for twenty dry years in that one day. They let Trinket cover her twice before they went up for their prayers and chicken and dumplings, and while they was eating, they was so ashamed and guilty they couldn't look at each other. Especially Eddie. Only then Mrs. Hood asked them if

they had give Birdie a bait of oats, and they said they had forgot, so she told them to get up right now and go do it, and this
time she give Eddie a whack on the head with her thimble as
he slid past her.

That put the iron in Eddie's soul for a while, and so they let
Trinket cover her twice more before they give Birdie her oats,
and this time they didn't have a bit of trouble handling Trinket,
he was an old hand at it. Then they hid out until it was time
to hitch up the mare for the Hoods to go home.

Now nobody is going to expect a mare twenty years old
to get with colt when she has never been bred before, especially from a little stud no bigger than a butchering calf. It
couldn't happen one time in a thousand, but this must of been
the thousandth time, because that's just what happened. Birdie
kept getting fatter and fatter, and Reverend Hood kept letting
out her bellyband, but nobody suspicioned the truth. Rolf and
Eddie kept track, and when July come, they both felt like running away from home and becoming train robbers, but they
couldn't bear to miss the fun.

One Wednesday there was a package for the Hoods from
a church they used to pastor back in Ohio, some free second-
hand clothes and crumbled cookies and so forth, and he had
to hitch up Birdie to go get it. He left her standing in front of
the post office, and while he was inside, she started to throw
her foal. Somebody seen what was happening, and even if he
couldn't believe it, he dropped her tugs and let her step ahead
so she wouldn't drop the colt on the singletrees. Sometimes a
mare takes a long time having a colt, but this was only a Shetland, and she got rid of it like spitting out a cherry pit.

A little spotted stud, the image of Trinket. She had done
had it, and half the town of Smith Center was standing around
watching it stumble to its feet and suck, when Reverend Hood
come out of the post office with his package. Old Birdie looked
just as proud as could be, throwing her head around at people
like she was saying, "You didn't think the old mare was up to
it did you, well now who's the fool, you or me?"

Reverend had two choices. Either his mare had had carnal

knowledge of a he-horse, or he had himself the first virgin birth of a horse in history. Well there was only one spotted stud in Smith County, and all anybody had to do was count back eleven months, and they could pin down the exact day. What made it worse was that his old mare fell from grace on a Sunday.

Eddie cried and said he was sorry, so their father only give him a couple of licks with a strap. But Rolf said he had been whacked once too often on the head with that Goddamn thimble, and he reckoned he had went insane, and he couldn't remember what happened. So he got two good larrupings, once for breeding the preacher's mare to the pony, and once for cursing and making light of it.

Reverend Hood come out of it all right in one way. He sold the colt as a two-year-old for seventy-five dollars, more cash than he had ever had in his hand since he got paid off from the Union Army, after laying in a stinking hospital outside of Washington for two months, after being shot in the knee at Fredericksburg.

He didn't even scold Rolf and Eddie, although he did talk to them. He said he didn't blame the horse and he didn't blame the pony, no, that was animal nature, they couldn't help themselves. But he said human beans could either yield to animal nature or conquer it, and they knowed that as well as he did. He reckoned boys had done worse things than this, only he said he couldn't figger out why they done this one to him. "Why, boys?" he said. "You knew it would humiliate me. If I could understand that—but you don't know yourselves, do you?" And they couldn't bring themselves to tell him about his wife whacking them on the head with her thimble, because she died not long after the colt was born, and before Reverend Hood got around to questioning them.

10

Rolf laid there in the hammock and tried to go back to sleep, but he couldn't get them Hoods off'n his mind. The Hoods raised a little patch of corn, and they had a coffee mill that they used to grind their meal in, and they said there just wasn't no meal like that you ground fresh before baking. But when Reverend Hood died, and they laid him out and seen how skinny he was, and they found only $2.08 in the whole house, and nothing in the cupboard but a little tea, the truth come out.

Them poor old people was hungry, that was why they went around mooching Sunday dinners, they prob'ly lived on cornbread and weak tea most of the week. The old woman whacked kids on the head with her thimble to let out her misery, where others would of took an ax and called attention to it by mass murder. No two ways about it, a retired preacher is a cast-off cull, unless he's managed to put out a little money on mortgages, or married it. And if he did, he's an object of revilement for serving Mammon, so he can't win.

Well not me, Rolf thought. I never felt no call to preach. I got caught in quicksand, and everybody pushed.

He made up his mind to get up there and preach them one more farewell sermon next Sunday, and apologize for taking up their time, and the next day he'd be on his way out of Colorado. He wouldn't even ride Fanny home, it was going to be too hard parting with that horse, but it was worth it to get rid of this load. And the next thing he was thinking was, Anyway how do I even know there is a God? If there was, what did He ever do for Reverend Hood?

Well then he heard a voice say, "What do you mean, cowboy? It's not what I done *for* him that really bothers you, it's what *you* done *to* him."

Rolf never claimed it was an out-loud voice that anybody could of heard. He knowed it was all in his own mind, but the funny thing was, when he looked away from that patch of blue sky he stopped hearing it, and when he looked back, here it was talking at him again. The wind had let up, and the leaves was still, and here was this little patch of blue. And being as he wasn't the kind to drop an argument with anybody, he made the most respectful reply he could, and it went about like this:

ROLF: You mean, Lord, that I'm not even with You yet for what I done to Reverend Hood?

THE LORD: The man was in his seventies. He may not have been the brightest vessel that ever bore My truth, but he fought the good fight and he kept the faith, and you crowned him with ridicule and humiliation.

ROLF: A joke is a joke, Lord. It wasn't all that bad.

THE LORD: Cowboy, when you're in your seventies, and standing in the only patched shoes you own, afraid to bend over because your pants are liable to bust, and you been on bread and tea for six days, wait until then and tell me if a joke is still a joke.

ROLF: Then how do I get square for what I done?

THE LORD: You'll know when you're forgiven, cowboy. You have to forgive yourself, that's about it.

ROLF: Well if You'll excuse me, Lord, it looks to me like I'm just heaping more ridicule and humiliation on Reverend Hood when I pretend to be a preacher myself.

THE LORD: That could be true, cowboy. You flourish around right smart, healing people, getting into fights and then comforting the loser, things like that. But I just wonder what's in your heart all this time.

ROLF: So do I. That's what bothers me, that's what I can't face up to, what business have I got preaching?

THE LORD: Yes, I can see how you'd wonder that.

ROLF: Getting back to Reverend Hood and his mare, I plead guilty to worse than just nasty, it was cruel to an old man and woman, but in all modesty, let me ask You this: Ain't I almost even after helping Lois out of her convulsion?

THE LORD: You may even be ahead of that game, cowboy. But when your heart tells you that you're forgiven for what you done to Reverend Hood, then you can start paying for the blessing that saved you from the gallows, or at least hatred and despair for life in prison. You was well on your way in that direction when My chaplain pulled you out of the Hole, and you know it as well as I do.

ROLF: You mean I've got to slash away at trying to preach here, until I pay off *all* of my debts?

THE LORD: Do what your heart tells you to do, cowboy. Why don't you want to do it?

ROLF: I'll turn my hand over face up, Lord. I can't get Abe Whipple or these other people to understand, but maybe You will. I didn't mind slopping around helping the chaplain in prison, anything you do there is better than nothing, and I did take babtism, and I'll go through with a deal I've made, clear to the line fence. But these people expect more, and Lord, they're *entitled* to more. It just seems I'll be forever, paying back in pennies for debts that I owe in dollars, don't You see what I mean?

THE LORD: You just bet I do, cowboy.

ROLF: Looks like a long job.

THE LORD: Oh no! You can get up out of that hammock and go do as you please, any time. Nothing's got you by the seat of your pants except your conscience.

ROLF: You know me better than that, Lord.

THE LORD: I thought I did, cowboy. I didn't think you'd let these people down.

ROLF: Well, Lord, I'll stay until they can rustle up a genuine preacher, how's that?

THE LORD: Suit yourself, cowboy.

ROLF: No sir, I'll try to suit You. I'll stay here a few more Sundays, and do my sincerest best to give these people what they're looking for, if they know what it is. I sure don't! Look at Alf Constable, already he unloaded a murder on me, how do I know what else I'm going to run into in this congregation of strays? You know what we get out here on the frontier, Lord! But if I've got it to do, I'll do the best I can.

THE LORD: That's all I asked of My own Son, cowboy.

11

That was something to sweat through, even if it was all in his mind, enough to make Rolf shun that hammock like it was full of bedbugs. Well then, when he come out from under them grapevines, after the wind swung around and started blowing from the hogpen, he blundered into the Constables' house and discovered a whole lot of company had come there, trapping him. And listening to them, he found out that the preacher was expected to put out *two* sermons every Sunday, one in the evening.

He didn't feel in shape for it, no he didn't, but he skimmed back and forth through his Bible, and he finely found something he reckoned he could whomp up a sermon on, "A new Commandment I give ye, that ye love one another." It prob'ly wasn't the best, because it's generally considered best for the Easter season, and here it was early summer, and besides, there is prob'ly more dirty cowboy jokes about love than anything else. But they told him he didn't need to worry, the evening crowd generally didn't amount to a hill of beans, mostly old maids or families with daughters they was trying to marry off, so not to worry.

They couldn't of been more wrong. Blessed Sacrament was only a mission, and Father Lavrens that run it had other flocks to herd, and this wasn't his Sunday in Mooney. And all of them sects had got careless about property lines anyway. Father Lavrens's bishop was always having him up for drumhead proceedings on the way his flock rambled after every whooping evangelist in forty miles, and one of the reasons Brother Richardson had finely hauled off and quit First Methodist was that every time Blessed Sacrament had a carnival, or a feast day, or any reason for trotting out the altar boys in their lace gowns, why the Methodist crowd thinned out, and everybody went to Blessed Sacrament to see the show. There was a good deal of ignorant discussion of doctrine, and now and then some intermarriage, and a general loosening of the laws of regularity, and the loss of money that goes with it. A person he's a guest in some other church, he feels called upon to be a little liberal about it, and he ponies up two bits instead of a dime, or four bits instead of two, and it really ain't fair. Suppose you owned a saloon, and your own bartender never touched the stuff on duty, but the minute his day was over, he went across the street and handed out a dime of your money for somebody else's whisky. You'd take offense too.

There was some French Kincaiders who come a long way to Mass, only to find out Father Lavrens wasn't in Mooney, most of them named Beauseigneur, pronounced Bossinner, but one family of Lally, and a few of other names, including one young single unmarried bachelor by the name of Bob Gaston. They all come to the Methodist church, and so did all four Venamans. The collection was $31.75, mighty good, plus a $1,000 check from Harold DuSheane. He was the town halfwit, and not French at all despite his name. He was perfectly harmless except that he'd take a leak just any old where, and was always writing them big checks. There was a few atheists too.

After the services, when the people marched out, them

Frenchmen all wanted to kiss Rolf's hand, and it was just short of a rassling match to keep them from doing it, and then this Bob Gaston wanted Rolf to interduce him to Samantha Venaman. He seemed to feel it was his duty. He spoke perfectly good English, and he said, "I'll go this far, Reverend, if anything comes of it, I won't bear down on her to join my church, I'll come a-helling to yours. Now is that a fair deal or ain't it?"

He couldn't get out of interducing her, and then he had to stand there part of the party while Cal tried to get away, and Samantha deviled him by shining up to this Frenchman, knowing how Cal felt about Frenchmen. Finely Bob asked Cal if he could call on Samantha, and Cal said, "I don't see how the hell I can prevent it if I can't even start for home," and the Frenchman took the hint and left.

Rolf thought he never seen Samantha look so pretty, after all that gushing from that Frenchman, and he was in a moody state of mind anyway. She said she could see that he had put a lot of thought into his sermon, and he said he didn't know whether to thank her for that or not, and she wanted to know why not.

He said, "Well, that's the kind of compliment your lawyer would pay the jury, after they come in with guilty. You've got to say something."

She laughed and said, "You're too sensitive, Reverend. When I vote to hang, no one is in doubt. No really, the highest compliment a preacher can pay his congregation is merely to *think*, and make them think too."

He said, "I hope somebody was thinking, man, because I was bogged down in the quicksands of indecision as the fella says, and I just couldn't find the words, I reckon because I wasn't sure what I was trying to get over."

She said, "Oh that was quite clear, but it's the seeking that counts, truth plays hide-and-seek with all of us, and we count on you for guidance—not answers so much as leadership in our seeking," and so on.

Cal said, "If you're through instructing our pastor, daughter, let's get along."

She fetched up short, and seen how excited she had got, and she must of thought it made her look foolish, but it wasn't in her to apologize, not ever. She'd stand pat on what she had dealt herself, that was her nature and nobody was going to change her.

Cal said, "Have you seen that nitwit sheriff, Parson? I expected him to be at services, but he's never around when you need him."

Rolf was still gaping at Samantha, and it took a minute for that to soak in. He said, "Has Abe done neglected you? That don't sound like Abe to me."

You can see how he was already getting the swing of being a minister, bringing peace and goodwill to his flock, instead of the normal human tendency to act the son of a bitch, just to see the fun.

Cal said, "Oh no, not much, my house is robbed, that's all!"

"Why," Rolf said, "I heard that Abe was out investigating a robbery."

Cal said, "He sure was, mine. I lost forty-eight hundred dollars in less than a year I figger, first my best hay-fat beef, and now sixteen hundred in gold. Abe came out and looked wise, and then went plodding off on his horse to look for tracks. About as much chance of him finding tracks as an elephant. They shot both of my dogs, too! Nobody could have gotten past my dogs. I had two of the best watchdogs in the country, and I regret them more than the money. They died for me, and redressing that is as important as getting back my money. You tell Abe I said that!"

Rolf said, "I thought you worked upwards of thirty or forty men, and now you tell me some of your beef was run off, and now your house is robbed. Where was your crew when your dogs was shot and your house was robbed?"

"Working, where they're supposed to be! I can account for every man I've got, Parson. No man of mine did it. Some two hundred head of prime steers vanished last winter, between snowstorms. Now they come into my very home. This isn't some hungry, out-of-work cowboy's work. It took a gang to do it after a leader planned it, and you can tell this distinguished Sephardic sheriff of ours that I said so," Cal said.

Opal said, "Reverend, Cal holds Abe responsible for everything from drouth to the bots, just because he supported him for sheriff. And he'll hold you responsible now too, because you're Abe's nominee. You may as well be prepared, you're expected to have at least five or six angels looking after Flying V interests."

Cal grinned like he had his temper back, and said, "Five or six, the dickens, I'm entitled to a squadron of them at least."

Rolf lost his head completely. He said, "Well, Mr. Venaman, you already have a couple of them, these two daughters, and I'll get you the rest of your ten thousand when you need them."

Samantha put out her hand without warning to shake hands good-by, and then Opal and Winnie, and then Cal, but you bet he didn't get no inspiration out of Cal's handshake. Cal said good-by, and he told Rolf, "Ten thousand, that's a lot of angels, you just conjure up one old loudmouthed sheriff, and I'll tie him to an anthill until he's paid in suffering for my two dogs."

They headed on home, and Rolf woke up and seen it was time to hunt up Jack Butler, only then this town halfwit, Harold DuSheane, come running to say he'd found Jack drownded in the crick. Jack wasn't drownded, only half so. He was upstream from the footlog a quarter of a mile, where nobody but a drunk would of been blundering around, and nobody but a halfwit could of found him.

They took him to Huey's place, and renched off the mud, and started pouring black coffee into him, and now and then they'd slap his face to bring the blood to his head, and pretty soon it was even money he was going to live.

Abe Whipple didn't get back into town until nigh midnight, just when Rolf was about to start home with Jack Butler. Abe said no, put it off until tomorrow, anyway Jack had soaked up so much he couldn't stand another drink, and he wanted to talk to Rolf. He took Rolf to Bad Lim's place, a Chinese place that put up a good bait of Chinese food for two bits, something Rolf had never et before.

"Once you give up wondering what that meat is in it, there ain't none better than the Chinese grub," Abe said. "I like it so well, I wonder if maybe I haven't got some oriental blood in me somewhere."

"It's possible," Rolf said. "The way I feel tonight, I wouldn't bet a plugged lead nickel on the chastity of my own grandmother."

Abe said, "I'm with you there, and I think I love my son of a bitching fellow man as much as the next man, or maybe more, and I include that sterling citizen and leading cattleman, Calvin Venaman. I'm glad I missed him. Cal's all right in his way. He'll set up all night with a man of his that gets sick, and pay for his doctors, and every man that dies on his place, he gets a place in the Flying V private graveyard. But when it comes to abusing an animal, there's no moderation in him. He'll favor the animal every time. I keep telling that fool kid deputy of mine, Thad Rust, he'd be better off to have himself gelded in the long run. He's just at the age, and so is Winnie, and one of these days they won't be able to help themselves, they'll just rip their clothes off and go to it. A rooster is a rooster and a hen is a hen, and nature will have its way."

"The Lord gives us power over our natures," Rolf said.

"A dime's worth of power and a dollar's worth of nature. You can't blame these kids. It's the wrong way to go at it, but with spring weather and the hot weather coming so close together, the strain don't let up until somebody's knocked up. Green as a gourd, that's the word for Thad, and you've got to look at the practical side too. If them kids do get married, Cal ain't going to be satisfied to have no son-in-law in a deputy's job, oh hell no, he'll run Thad against me for my job, and them Rusts breed like flies. They're related to the Cooks and the Vandermeers and the Spurlings and Januarys and Warnocks, and what you've got to watch out for in politics is what they call a natural coalition. This one is so natural it would curl your hair," Abe said.

Rolf asked him what he found out about Cal's house robbery, and Abe got sick at his stomach, and shook his head a long time, and said, "Not a thing, not a damn thing. I'm in trouble, Rolf, plenty of trouble! This ain't no little old two-bit hometown robber gang. We're close to Nebraska and close to Wyoming, and it looks to me like somebody from one of them two states is coming down here and helping himself to our wealth. State lines are a damn nuisance, Rolf. We didn't used to pay no attention to them, you lined out chasing your desperado, and you run him till you caught him, and you hung him on the spot, and that was that. I never knowed of no foreign sheriff from the other state interfering, and I never interfered when they trailed their horse thieves down here, and believe you me we had law and order. Now it's all law and no order."

Rolf said he wished he had Thad's job instead of the one he had, and any time Abe had a vacancy, he wanted to be considered for it. Abe said no sir, where Rolf was now was where he was needed; anybody could be a deputy sheriff with a little training, but preaching took special talents that you didn't pick off'n every bush.

"Well I ain't going to stay with it, and you might as well get used to it, Abe," Rolf said. "I'll be on my way soon, I reckon. Soon as they can rustle up another preacher, be he good, bad, or indifferent."

"What in thunderation has got into you?" Abe wanted to know. "I swear, you ain't the same boy I last seen!"

Rolf said no, he sure wasn't, and Abe asked him what had happened, and Rolf said he didn't care to talk about it, and Abe said he could understand that and he didn't want to pry, but it worried him when a man got that dreened-out look in his eyes that Rolf had. So Rolf said it was partly Samantha Venaman, he was afraid he was getting to be a goner for her, and he knowed what chance an ex-convict preacher had with her, but that wasn't really what had changed his mind. Abe kept after him, kept sidling and circling and backing around, and he had a lot of practice in snaking your soul out backward, he'd get the kernel out without cracking the nut, and that's what he done to Rolf. Pretty soon, Rolf was telling him about laying there in the hammock at Alf's place, and carrying on the most logical and lifelike conversation with God you ever heard of, and he didn't expect Abe to believe him, but he'd had a revelation that proved he wasn't fit to preach and would go on doing it at peril of his immortal soul.

Abe said, "Well, maybe it was a daydream and maybe it wasn't, I'll bet you won't find it in no dream books, but if you're asking me do I think you've went insane, why no I don't. I reckon it was like when Moses went up there on Sinai, he purely had to be by hisself a while to cipher things out, them people of his'n was enough to drive a steady man frantic, and Moses never did seem to me very steady. A drifter, not satisfied no place. He may of been a prophet, but any man that can ramble for forty years, he's got to be unsteady, Rolf, he's *got* to be! I don't mean an unsteady man can't be a prophet, no sir, but I ain't going to take an unsteady man's literal word necessarily, either. I reckon he went up there on the mountain, and hid out from them people before they drove him plumb out of his mind, and set down on a rock, and said to himself, 'Moses, look here, you ain't getting nowhere with these folks, and there has to be a reason, and until you know what's wrong, how are you going to figure out what to do?' Like you done there in the hammock. Well it come to him what was wrong, them people didn't have no *rules;* they believed in the One and Only God true enough, that's all right, I don't quarrel with that, but a God without rules might as well not be God at all. So he come up with these rules, and he laid them out simple and stiff, there it is, take it or leave it, foller the rules or get out of the tribe. He had to stretch it a little when he come down from Sinai, and give yourself credit, Rolf, *you* didn't, you told her just the way she happened to you, no blast of thunder and fire, and no carved stones either. It's the difference in times, see. We're ignorant enough here on the frontier, but we ain't a caution to them people. Why they even had a rule to cut the end of your pecker off, I reckon because it got dirty on them, and it's mighty skeerce getting a bath in the desert. Well that's all right as a last resort, but a man can spit on it and keep it clean, why trim it off?

You can't blame Moses for telling a stretcher to people like that. They was just a bunch of blanket Indians on the warpath, looking for somebody they could whip, and take his land away from him, and rustle his cattle. And I'll tell you something else, Rolf, except that some of us can read and write, and we don't mutilate ourselves except in fights, *we ain't a Goddamn bit better today!*"

"You're sure in a cheerful state of mind, Abe," Rolf said. "A man comes to you already feeling low, and you send him away fit to cut his own throat."

"Well it's the truth!" Abe said. "I'll tell you what I think, the time is coming when people are going to look back on us and say, 'My God, and they called themselves civilized!' and they'll be right! Look at us, shooting each other, and cutting each other with knives, and hanging each other, why if you see a man going around unarmed, you know he's either a preacher or drunk or lost it in a game somewhere, and you call that civilized. Look at the way we treat our women! Edna has got it pretty good now, compared to some women I know, but I knowed the time she was no better than a pack animal, same as most women on the frontier, before I woke up and said to myself, let the Goddamn county support us! What has a woman in this country got to look forward to? The whores is the lucky ones, at least they price their own ass, that's something, but the average rancher's wife is just livestock. Have her babies alone on a dirty old straw tick, and try to make milk in her breasts for them from nothing but beans and hog meat and corn meal, no beef for her, oh no, the Goddamn beef has all got to be shipped and sold! And a Kincaider's wife is even worse off, you might as well hitch her to the plow with your ox and be done with it. Their kids grow up mean and wild, all wanting to be train robbers, all packing guns from the time they're thirteen, and not worth the powder to blow them to hell. When there's no hope for the young people except raising hell and shooting and peddling their ass, your country's on the road to ruin. The time is coming, and you mark my words, Rolf, that people are going to look back and say one and all that this was the worst part of the history of mankind, and the cowboy was the lowest, meanest thing that ever walked on two legs, and yet you want to go back to riding for a living!"

"You sure can cheer a man up," Rolf said.

Abe said, "Don't take it so personal. It's just that I hate to see a young fella ruin his life twice."

"I can't be a hypocrite."

"You could if you tried. It only takes a little. Look at Moses. The thing that's important ain't whether the Lord dynamited them stone tablets out for him personally, it's the rules that count. Rolf, this here country is about as lean and raw and worthless as the Holy Land was then. It's got a little more water, but not much, and a little more grass, but not much, and about the same kind of people. But the Lord valued that property enough to send His angels down there again and again, to line them ungrateful fools up, and to help them against the Hittites and the Assyrians and all them other worthless tribes. Now if He thought that much of a few acres of stony old desert, how can you just ride out of here and completely abandon and desert a country that needs you as bad as this country does?"

"I never seen no angels of the Lord around here," Rolf said. "I don't think this is angel range, Abe."

Abe just glared at him. "If there's one thing I can't stand, it's a smart-aleck, but go ahead, be a cowboy, and may the Lord have mercy on your ignorant soul!"

"Amen," Rolf said.

12

Rolf and Jack got a late start back to the ranch the next day, because Jack had the bull-shakes and the whisky trots, and couldn't trust himself on a horse. Rolf was pretty impatient with him, and he rode Fanny as hard as he thought Jack could foller, and he had him in pretty good shape by the time they got home. Jack had bought two gunnysacks full of groceries and stuff, and when they got home he dumped them in a corner, and said he believed he'd turn in and get some sleep.

"Oh no you don't," Rolf said. "You and me are going to build some fence, and sweat some of the whisky out of you."

Jack said, "The hell with that, I'm sick as a dog, and if there's one man in Colorado caught up on his fences, I'm that man, and whoever said work is the healer never felt like I do." But Rolf made him go out and help as long as he could, which was only until about noon. Jack seen by the shadows that it was midday, and he said he hadn't et nothing for thirty-six hours, so Rolf let him quit, and they both went in. Rolf took care of the team, and when he come into the house, Jack had unpacked the groceries, and was standing there staring at them.

"What do you call this?" he said.

Rolf said, "Why, I'd call that a quart of Tom Sanderson's Old Bluetick sourmash whisky thirteen years in the wood. Jack, you have run from that stuff long enough. That bottle is going to stand there on the table and reproach you. Any time you feel like taking a drink, tell me about it man to man, and I'll help you stave it off. If that don't work, we'll try something else."

"That sure is hospitality to your worst enemy," Jack said, "but we'll do it your way. No danger now, I can tell you! The very idee gives me nowsea."

For three days that black bottle set on that table, with the picture of that bluetick hound on it. Jack got up in the morning talking about it, and he talked about it while they worked, and while they et dinner, and all afternoon, and at supper too, and it was the last thing he mentioned at night.

The evening of the third day, Jack took a bucket and went down to the horse tank and had a bath, and stropped up his razor and shaved himself, and put on some new Levis he got out of the drawer of his dresser, and a new white shirt too. Rolf said, "What in the world do you aim to do with all of them clothes? Why you've got enough clothes there for a store!"

"I like to be well dressed when I go out," Jack said, "and I'm always losing clothes, or getting them tore up or filthy dirty when I'm drunk."

"Where do you think you're going now?" Rolf said.

"You expect too much of me. I can't set there and look at that bottle and grit my teeth. I've got to get out of here, that's all," Jack said.

"Where to?" Rolf asked him.

"Nowhere. Anywhere. A long hard punishing ride to get my mind off'n the drink," Jack said.

"You didn't need to clean up for that. You're heading back to Mooney," Rolf said.

Jack swore he wasn't, he just felt unclean with a fit coming on, but Rolf said to set down, they was going to start talking this thing out.

"I won't set down and I won't talk," Jack said. "I'm so nervous I could scream, so don't push at me!"

"Then get down on your knees and we'll ask the Lord's help," Rolf said.

"I don't want His help, He'll only say torture myself for greater glory, and glory is something I can do plumb without," Jack said.

"All right, you won't set, and you won't talk, and you won't pray, all right, go ahead and drink. Here, I'll pull the cork for you, so's you can smell it," Rolf said, and he did.

"Don't try to shame me, Rolf. I'm past shame," Jack yelled.

Rolf unbuttoned his shirt and peeled it off, and he advised Jack to do the same. Jack asked why, and Rolf said, "Because you and me and your demon is going down into a tangle over your immortal soul, winner take all this time."

"What do you aim to do?" Jack wanted to know.

"See you get your fill of whisky for once," Rolf said.

"You are like hell! You're fired. Get off'n my place!" Jack hollered.

Rolf come at him, and he had an advantage not having any shirt for Jack to get hold of. Jack wasn't a big man, but he was hard-built and quick on his feet, and he put up a pretty fair scrap. But Rolf got him down on his back, dead to the world from a clip on the jaw, and was setting there on top of him when he come to. Rolf had the bottle in his hand, and as soon as he seen that Jack was awake, he tipped it into his mouth.

"Drink or drownd, you miserable sinner!" he said, and kept it there until Jack begin to lose it out of the corner of the mouth, and waste that good whisky. Rolf let him get his breath again, and then it was "Drink or drownd, you miserable sinner!" again. That system is calculated to take a lot of the pleasure out of getting drunk, and Jack finely passed out without ever getting more than relief, no enjoyment at all.

Rolf put the bottle on the table, where Jack could find it when he come to, if he did, and then a rider from Elias Petty's little Lion Track ranch galloped up, and he said that Mrs. Petty's aged mother, Mrs. Urma Perkins, was dying and wanted to be comforted going over the hump. Miz Urma, as they called her, was in her eighties, and had come to Colorado in a covered wagon pulled by a span of good brindle Ohio oxen, and had been burnt out by Indians twice and scalped once, so she had this little bare pucker on top of her head where there wasn't no hair. She was originally a deep-dip Babtist, but had went to the Methodist until she got too feeble, and was entitled to all the privileges of a communicant member.

Rolf loaded his books into his saddlebags, and they went out on a gallop, and Rolf got to the Lion Track in time to give the old lady a boost when she needed it, and she died full of grace. It was coming on to rain then, so they hitched up a team and wrapped the remains in quilts and put them on the bed of a wagon, because she wanted to be buried in town. Well then when they got to town, Bernard Petty, the embalmer, a cousin of Elias, said there wasn't no use embalming the old lady, it was too hard to find her veins, and anyway people as old as her was so dried-up they didn't rot, they couldn't for lack of juices. All they done was sort of tan like a cowhide; however, it was hot weather, and a good idee to conduct the burial with all decent haste.

So Rolf conducted the funeral, and used the Book of Common Prayer again, and enough of Miz Urma's kin showed up on short notice to make a nice walking cortege, and the rain held off. About midnight, the Lion Track bunch started home, because they had left some wash on the line, and Rolf thought he might as well go back to the lonely bachelor quarters he shared with Jack.

When he got there, he found Jack gone, and his new clothes in a pile in the middle of the floor, all over puke, and the bottle missing, and so was Jack's saddle. Rolf went to bed, not as worried as he might of been, because as the saying is, the Lord takes care of children and drunks. He slept late, until almost six o'clock, and then a bunch of Flying V boys rode in and wanted to borrow all of Jack's wagons.

Jack only had two, and he wasn't around anywhere to say aye, yes or no, but Rolf told them go ahead, help themselves. The Flying V boys had brought along extra harnessed teams to pull the wagons with. Rolf thought it was kind of curious that Cal Venaman would need extra wagons, so he asked why.

One of these riders said, "Why the Q mixed train went on the ground, a real interesting wreck, and Cal usually gets the job of teaming and hauling whenever they have a wreck or a washout on the line."

Rolf said, "Then if he's going to be paid in cash, he can pay cash rental for them wagons, and you tell him I said that."

This rider, he said it was unneighborly to take that attitude, but he'd tell Cal; however, they'd always borried Jack's wagons before and never had this question come up, and Rolf said, "That's a rich man for you. To them that have shall be given, well I reckon not in this case, somebody's got to take care of that poor sot's interests."

They went off with them two wagons, and Jack finely come in an hour or two later, looking like the wrath of God, and unable to tell where he'd been or what he'd done, only that by now it was clear that a long hard punishing ride wasn't the answer to his problem. He set there holding his head and saying, "Oh God oh God oh God oh God," and then he'd jump up and throw hisself at the door and try to puke, and couldn't, and then he got to seeing lizards all over everything. Not snakes but lizards. He'd scream, "There they are, coming down from the ceiling on that rope, swat the shiny green sonsabitches somebody, oh my God cut that rope, they're all over me, I got shiny green lizards down my shirt collar," and so on.

It was an original change from snakes, but a drunk is a drunk and that's about all you can say for them, so when Jack finely went to sleep on the kitchen floor, Rolf totted it up in his mind and concluded he'd lost this bout with the devil for good. He packed up all of his few belongings, and left a little note for Jack saying he was quitting and that he had loaned his wagons to Cal Venaman, and got on his horse and rode out of there.

He went up north to the Q to see this wreck first, and it was an interesting one all right. The engine was still standing, but it was astraddle of one rail and could of tipped over pretty easy, and the combination passenger and baggage and mail car was on its side, and so was two box cars. This was a swampy stretch of track built up on a fill, and they had to put in a rip-

track detour around it, to get trains through, and to let the
wrecker come in and set the wrecked train up again.

Cal had seven teams hauling dirt in wagons, and five teams
on grading slips, and was setting on his horse making sure
they put out a day's work and didn't abuse his horses. He
nodded to Rolf and said, "So I'm expected to pay Jack rent on
his wagons, am I? I've never had this demand made on
me before, Parson."

Rolf said, "It's up to Jack. I was responsible at the time, and
I thought it was the fair thing to do. If Jack don't want pay,
it's nothing to me."

"So I'm a rich man, am I?" Cal said. "You know of course
that I have to pay Liz Saymill six hundred dollars every quarter, if you don't you're the only man in Mooney County that
don't, old bigmouth Abe Whipple saw to that. I'll tell you
how that verse really ought to go, Parson, to them that has
shall be given trouble and taxes, until all they have is taken
away from them, and then some."

"As I said, fix it up with Jack," Rolf said.

"Mighty decent of you, Parson, I appreciate your attitude,"
Cal said, and rode off a little ways where Rolf couldn't talk
to him no more.

It really put a chill on Rolf to be treated like that by the
father of Samantha Venaman, and yet he didn't see how he
could of done any different about the wagons. Four bits a day
for a wagon, or a dollar for both, wasn't going to break Cal, it
wasn't bean soup to the six hundred dollars he had to pay
Liz Saymill every three months, and yet it would mean a lot
to a poor man like Jack Butler, because a thirst like Jack's was
as expensive to support as a family. It was the same old thing
Rolf had seen all his life, people in Cal's position expected too
much of people in Jack's position, and Rolf's position. They
took it as their right, and a cowboy with nothing in his pocket
could say yes sir you bet sir or get out of the way, and it was
the same with the preacher. Cal would let the church board
fool around for a while, even let them hire a preacher without
consulting him, but he'd pull them up short when he took the

notion, because in his mind he run that church the same as he run the Flying V.

No, no question about it, he had let Rolf know where he stood, partly because Rolf was Abe Whipple's friend and he blamed Abe for his troubles, and partly because Rolf had the gall to ask him to pay for Jack's wagons, when the sot ought to be grateful for a chance to loan them. So Rolf headed toward Mooney, pushing his old worthless horse right along, and saying to himself, Well this does it, I give it a try, it could of been some good experience for me but I done everything wrong, like I always do.

He couldn't feel the presence of the Lord at all that morning, and he couldn't of prayed if somebody had put a gun at his head, and in a way it was a relief because now the strain was over. He could go get a job riding somewhere, and slide back into cursing and drinking and fighting a little at a time, and never get as obnoxious as he used to be, and stay out of prison this time. But at least have some fun out of life.

But a man can plan all he wants, and there's still times that circumstances does the deciding for him, and this was one. He was still three miles out of Mooney when here come a spring wagon at a good hard gallop towards him from town, and he pulled up and said to himself, Say now, I've seen that team before!

And he had, because it was the good Flying V buggy team pulling the spring wagon, and it was Winnie Venaman and Thad Rust in it eloping. Winnie broke out crying, she was so glad to see him, and Thad almost cried too. He had run them good buggy horses of Cal's until they was lathered and winded and wouldn't answer the whip no more, and he had a crick in his neck from looking back expecting to see Cal coming after them with both guns blazing.

"You've got to marry us, Reverend," he said. "You're our last hope. Oh my God, if that old fire-breathing daddy of hers catches us before it's legal, why I'm as good as a dead man."

"I don't see how I can do it," Rolf said. "I don't owe Cal

Venaman anything, but I can't do something like this behind his back, either."

"You'll never do it any other way," Thad said.

"Please, please, *please*, Reverend," Winnie said, and cried harder. "Do I have to shame myself and spell it out for you? I missed my time this month, and Thad will marry me, that's a lot more than most men would do, but Papa will just kill him if he finds out."

Rolf said he wasn't no expert, but it seemed to him he'd heard that a woman could miss her time for other reasons than the one she mentioned, however that did put a different light on things. Them kids had done just about everything else wrong too. They had went to the courthouse before Earl Sheffield, the county clerk, got his hind end out of bed, and Minnie Newhouse was the only person there. Minnie was deputy clerk, deputy treasurer, deputy registrar of deeds, and deputy everything else. She was getting on in years, and was kind of deef, and maybe a mite foolish. She forgot to ask about parents' consent, and anyway she knowed that Winnie was above the age of consent, so she wrote them out a license to marry.

There was a justice of the peace, Ed DuSheane, father of the town halfwit and some other kids, but he had went to Colorado Springs about an old family lawsuit there, and the county judge, Andy Obers, was a personal and political friend of Cal Venaman's, and the Catholic priest, Father Lavrens, wouldn't of married a couple of Protestants even if he'd been in town.

The truth was, Rolf was their last hope unless Winnie had missed her time for some other reason, and the odds was against that, and to tell the truth, Rolf wasn't in no particular mood by then to consider Cal Venaman's pride anyways. Not after the way Cal had treated him over that proposition of paying rent for Jack's wagons.

So they turned the spring wagon around, and they went into Mooney together with Rolf plodding his old horse alongside, and they went to Liz Saymill because Rolf thought she would be more independent of what Cal might think and do about it. She was all right, it just pleased her like nothing on earth to be asked to hold the wedding, and she went out and rustled up another old maid for a witness, and Rolf got the Bible and the Book of Common Prayer out, and married them there in the parlor where Colonel Pegler T. Saymill had been murdered. He filled out the certificate and signed it as the officiating clergyman, and then he asked what the kids planned to do while Cal was getting used to the idea.

"Don't ask that question, because if you don't know the answer, you won't be held accountable," the bridegroom said.

Rolf said all right, he wouldn't ask it, but he heard about it later. The kids knowed about a nice cabin out in the willer brush along the creek, down in the homestead country closer to the Platte. There was an old Kincaider, Luke Sweeney, who lived there first, before he bought up some other homesteads and built a bigger house, and he ran a few steers and done a little farming, and made a little white whisky that he sold privately. He was a sort of anarchist anyway, and didn't care what Cal Venaman or any other person in authority thought, and wouldn't even vote.

They rented the cabin for a week, and had Luke bring them some groceries. Luke had a boy of eleven, Grover, who was learning to play the cordeen, and the family made him take it out in the willers to practice it, so they couldn't hear him. But if they couldn't, the happy young couple could. This kid Grover had learned to play several songs, and he had one song he was learning to sing while he played it, and this was what he was working on at the time. They heard it so often they got to know it too, and it went like this:

> I went to the river
> And I couldn't get across,
> So I paid five dollars
> For an old gray hoss.
> The hoss wouldn't go,
> So I traded for a hoe.

The hoe wouldn't dig,
So I traded for a pig.
The pig wouldn't squeal,
So I traded for a wheel.
The wheel wouldn't run,
So I traded for a gun.
The gun wouldn't shoot,
So I traded for a boot.
The boot wouldn't wear,
So I traded for a bear.
The bear wouldn't holler,
So I traded for a dollar.
The dollar wouldn't pass,
So I flung it in the grass.

Grover got up early to practice, and in the evening after he had did his milking and unharnessed the teams and got the cobs in for the stove the next day, he went out into the willers and practiced again, and if a dog started a bobcat or a coon and got to baying at night and woke him up, he'd grab that cordeen and head for the willers to practice, or any reason. Luke said if that kid was as dedicated to a harrow or scythe as he was the cordeen, he'd be a big property owner someday. But a happy young couple on a honeymoon, they don't object to being woke up early in the morning, or in the middle of the night, or any old time for that matter; they just kept the shades pulled down and let him holler and play the cordeen all he liked. For years after that, every time Thad and Winnie heard that song, they'd clasp hands and just sigh all over the place. It got to be their song, you might say.

13

Cal didn't miss Winnie until late that afternoon. Winnie told her mother she was going berry-picking, and she took a pail out, and she hitched up the buggy team to the spring wagon because she knowed Cal would have a fit if she drove the good buggy out there in the rocks to the berry patch, and where she made her mistake was in leaving her berry pail in the barn. Cal didn't have no way of knowing she was a sort of a have-to case, but he figgered from the first she had run off with Thad, and all he wanted was to get her back and kill Thad.

Tired as he was from the train wreck, Cal rode into town with a dozen of his boys, looking for her. He looked for Abe Whipple first, but Abe had rode up to the train wreck to investigate it, although as Cal said what business it was of his how many trains the Q wrecked, he didn't know, and then he run into Earl Sheffield, the county clerk, on the street. Earl said he hadn't issued no marriage license to Winnie and Thad or to nobody else, business was bad in that line, and so far this year death certificates was thirteen to ten over marriage licenses, divorces far behind with only one so far, and births leading everything with eighteen.

Cal said he didn't trust any son of a bitch who had had his head in the public trough as long as Earl, so he went down to the courthouse to see for himself, and there was the record of the license Minnie had issued, and the certificate of marriage that Rolf had filed. The question now was whether to hunt up the minister and kill him, or go after the runaways. He couldn't find nobody that had seen which way the kids went when they left town, at least anybody that would talk. So it was the preacher's turn.

Cal started out to the J Bar B, not knowing that Rolf had quit there, with his cowboys behind him. About five minutes after he left, Abe come into town from investigating the train wreck, to say it was a busted rail that had throwed the train off. There was plenty of people to tell him that Cal Venaman had been in town looking for Reverend Ledger, to kill him for marrying Thad and Winnie, only they hadn't found him yet.

Abe was tired too, but he started out to the J Bar B to keep the peace, only he happened to think of looking in the church first just for luck, and there was Rolf's old bony horse tied behind it, and when he went in, there was Rolf setting in a pew staring at nothing. Abe went in and set down beside him and said, "Well, saying farewell to it all, I reckon," and Rolf said that was about the size of it, his one folly had been to tackle preaching in the first place, but he kind of liked this dark old building at that.

Abe said, "Well it'll miss you too, Rolf. I'm one of them people that believe that people leave their mark on a building, and this gloomy old place will be a little different because it was your church for a while, and my only regret is that some otherwise good memories has to be discolored by quitting under fire."

"What do you mean under fire?" Rolf said, and Abe told him about Cal Venaman going around looking for him to kill him. Rolf said that was just talk; one of the curses of the frontier was that people were always going to kill somebody, only usually they never did, and even when they did, he never heard of a preacher being killed. Cal would think twice.

"I ain't worried about Cal," Abe said. "I'll put an ax handle on his pulley and run his belt off, but it don't sound good for the church, no it don't; you'd never catch Father Lavrens leaving Blessed Sacrament under threat of death, now there's a man who'd just as soon be a martyr as not, poor old frail narrow-minded man."

Rolf said a Methodist made just as good a martyr as a Catholic any day if it came to that, not that he took any great stock in martyrdom as a blessing, it seemed to him more sensible to skin through somehow and go on serving the Lord alive. Abe said then there was Samantha, now *there* was martyrdom for you, she'd really catch it from Cal now.

Rolf said well, he wasn't in no particular hurry and he didn't like to run out on the church, and he might stay a couple of weeks just to prove his point, so Abe said let's go find him a place to stay.

There was two women that took in visiting missionaries, one a widow, Mrs. Rachel Wyatt, and one an old maid, Thea Pickering, who had been the other old maid that stood up with Thad and Winnie at their wedding. Rachel had the biggest house and was the best cook, but she had this daughter Lettie, about thirty-five and still single, and hell-bent on helping some man of God to discipline his congregation. Lettie wasn't ugly, or deformed, or anything like that, she was just too eager. You let a clerical male man get within a mile, and she started rolling her eyes and getting red-faced, and heaving her bosom, and she really had one to heave. There was some old talk that a visiting middle-aged missionary from the Ivory Coast had found her in his bed in the middle of the night when she was only fifteen, and before he knowed what to do about it he had already done it, and this was why her father had hung himself to a pear tree in the back yard.

The worst problem at Thea Pickering's place was her cats, seven or eight of them, and all over the house. But they was safer for a single unmarried bachelor clergyman than Lettie Wyatt, so Abe took him there. A little later, when Thea and Rolf was having supper, Abe brought Opal and Samantha Venaman there, so Rolf could assure them that Winnie was not living in sin somewhere.

"It's as legal as I could make it, ma'am," Rolf said. "They had the license, and they claimed there was no impediments, and I performed it before two witnesses, the way it said on the back of the certificate."

"I'm so glad!" Opal said.

"Well I'm glad you feel like that," Rolf said. "I hear your husband is having a fit, though."

"Yes, and he has had so many reverses lately. Money you know, and he has been stolen blind. He's a proud man, and these are hard blows," Opal said.

"He's a stiff-necked man," Rolf said. "Come now and let us reason together, that's still a good motto."

Opal laughed and said that was one way of looking at it, and too bad the people that run off their cattle and killed their dogs and robbed their house didn't feel the same way. She said that Samantha had a personal problem she wanted to talk over with him if he had the time, and she'd just wait in the buggy out in front until Samantha came out if Rolf had the time for her. So he said sure, if she thought her husband wouldn't object, and want to kill him twice.

Opal went out, and Rolf and Samantha set there a minute, and finely he said, "Was it about your sister, Miss Samantha? Because I don't know what I could tell you that I haven't already told you." He wasn't going to be the one to break the news that she had missed her time, and was going to come up with an eight-months grandchild to plague Cal still more.

Samantha said, "Oh no, I'm glad for her sake. I was in school with Thad, you know, and I'm not critical of him. It has been my observation that men have to go through a period of aimless, witless, worthless male lunacy. Thad may come out of it. I suppose Winifred's pregnant."

Well Rolf just turned red as a beet at that word. It would knock him over coming from anybody in mixed company, and Samantha just out with it like it was any old word, and the word didn't bother her and neither did her sister being in that condition.

She said, "No, I want to ask your frank opinion on the Catholic faith. Of converting."

That hit him harder than pregnant. He said, "Lord God of hosts, are you thinking of that?" and she said yes she was, and he said why it was worse than what Winnie had done, she might as well of got married.

She said, "Only no one asked me to do that, and the Catholic Church does ask all of us to unite with it."

He said, "It sure does, Miss Samantha, but it's a hard old row to hoe, and you've got your daddy's headstrong nature. In fact, you're as much like him as your sister is like your mother, come to think of it."

She said, "Thank you for your frankness although I'm not sure how you meant it. Certain things about the Catholic religion bewilder me, certain things repel me, and certain things attract me strongly. I might even think of becoming a nun."

"Lord God of hosts!" was all Rolf could say. "I must say, Miss Sammie, that when you say you've got a problem to talk over with the preacher, you come up with a dandy."

She said, "Well what do you think? And please don't call me Sammie, I hate that name."

He just couldn't stand the idea of this girl going for being a nun, and wearing that burlap underwear they're supposed to wear, and shaving their heads, and having to get up and pray on a stone floor so often, and like that. And yet he didn't feel like the kind of a fatherly old preacher that ought to be handling a proposition like this anyway. But she had asked him the question, and he just told himself that by George, he was going to give her the straightest answer he could.

"What I think," he said, "is that you hate too many things beside your nickname. Hate is a bad word for a Christian to point around recklessly, loaded or unloaded. Instead of arranging your life around what you hate, you ought to start thinking about the things you love for a change."

She said, "Oh indeed," and he said, "Well that's how I feel," and she said, "I see that I have wasted your time, I apologize, good night."

She jumped up and retch for her shawl, which had dropped to the floor while she was being so enthusiastic about being a nun, and he leaned over for it at the same time, and they knocked heads hard enough to put them both on the floor if either one of them had of been soft-headed. They stood up, each of them holding onto the shawl, a sort of brownish-gray one with a fringe she had knitted herself, and Rolf realized he hadn't seen her from this close before. In fact he hadn't seen *any* woman from this close since going to prison.

He said, "Miss Sammie, I reckon I barely know you, and shouldn't make judgment, but it seems to me there is nothing on earth you couldn't do if you set your heart to it. You've got the mind, and you've got the courage, and you ought to be the happiest person on earth, seems to me. All you have to do is just let yourself be yourself."

"What good does it do," she said, "when other people won't be their own selves?"

She was kind of squeaky-voiced and saucer-eyed, and he knowed it wasn't no spiritual problem that had drove her to this. No sir, this was just the way her sister had looked this morning. He said, "Say, is it this Bob Gaston that has caused this onset of interest in the Catholic faith? Because he told me he was willing to turn Methodist, the dirty double-crosser!"

She just looked at him awhile, and he could hear the old clock ticking away, and Aunt Thea's, as they called her, cats prowling around the back door wanting to be let in. And then she said, "No, it isn't Bob, although he has come to call on me, and that's a novelty if nothing else. Reverend Ledger, I'll presume to advise *you*, if I may. The next time a young woman comes to you with a problem, don't compliment her on her mind and her courage."

"I don't know anything better than them," Rolf said.

"Neither do I," said Samantha, "or I'd use it. Good night, Reverend Ledger."

Abe Whipple knowed Cal and his rowdies would be back in town soon, and they was. He heard them pound in at a gallop, and he began to meander over there to see what they had in mind, or thought they had in mind. But just then, here came

Opal and Samantha in the buggy, on their way back from their visit to the preacher.

Them women heard the Flying V riders too, there couldn't of been anybody in a mile that didn't hear that bunch clatter up, and nobody had to tell them what the next move was. They'd go after Rolf sure. Well just then they seen the sheriff, so Samantha hauled in on the lines and hollered "Whoa," and Opal sang out Abe's name, and he come over to the buggy in the dark.

Opal's teeth were just about chattering, she was that scared. She said, "That's Cal and the boys just got back, that bunch of riders, I reckon."

"I reckon," Abe said.

"He's looking for Reverend Ledger," Opal wept.

"I reckon," Abe grunted.

"Oh, Abe, he's out of his mind!" she said.

"Well I ain't out of mine," Abe said. "I declare, what's in that white kittle between your feet, Opal?"

"That?" she said. "Oh we had some chickens on frying for supper, and then when Cal took off with the men, without even coming to the house, we didn't want to stay to eat. We just put it in the kettle and brought it along."

"Well say! I wonder if you could spare an old man a wing, or something," Abe said. "I been so busy today I ain't hardly had time to eat. Don't you worry about Cal. He ain't going to breach the peace in *my* town."

They told him to help himself, and he took a couple of drumsticks and a couple of wings and his favorites, the gizzards. He went over to his house and got a couple of .30-30 lever-action rifles, and a 12-gauge shotgun, and a 16, and ammunition for all of them. So when Cal picked up the news that Rolf was boarding with Aunt Thea Pickering, and came riding with his crew to take him out and horsewhip him, here was Abe standing in the middle of the road with two .45's on him and a .30-30 under his arm, eating away at fried chicken from his shirt pocket.

"Now listen, I won't stand in the way of anybody who feels

there's a principle at stake," Abe said, "but if any of you twenty-five-dollar-a-month Ulysses Simpson Grants think you're going to abuse a man who never done you no harm, you're going to find out you're only George Armstrong Custers after all, with a Crazy Horse behind every horse turd. Cal, you ignorant son of a bitch, why can't you fight your own fights and not try to get a bunch of well-meaning cowpokes shot or jailed?"

This is what cold raw nerve can do. They woke up that they was only getting twenty-five dollars a month for risking their blood needlessly, and it wasn't their blood that was going to be mingled with that of Thad Rust and his tribe, and there just wasn't no way they could break even. That war party just faded away on the spur of the moment.

"I'll remember this to my dying day, Abe," Cal said. "I'm not a forgiving man, not where my family is concerned."

"Don't tell me your troubles, I'm not your rabbi," Abe said.

"What do you mean, rabbi?" Cal said.

"A rabbi is a minister to the Jews, and I'm part Spanish Jew, but I'm only a sheriff, not a rabbi. I can keep peace in the town, and don't you ever dream otherwise, but nobody can bring peace to that miserable worthless cinder you call a heart," Abe said.

It just made him sick, because he knowed he was through as sheriff with this term. He could look fur enough ahead to know that Winnie and her father was going to make up, it always happens that way, and then instead of killing Thad, Cal was going to try to figure out some way his ignorant worthless son-in-law could make a decent living for his wife and baby. And there was only one thing Thad knowed, sheriffing, and his tribe had the votes, and it was one of them natural coalitions instinct told Abe to fear. Abe could always make a little money cleaning out livery barns and so on, and sleep any old where, and he was bound to make out for himself. But it was a rough deal to put on Edna in their sunset years, and no consolation that he had brought it on her through devotion to duty. Women don't take duty and things like that as seriously as men do.

14

It seemed to him it hadn't no more than started to get day-light, and he'd barely been to sleep, when here they was, pounding on his door again. But Abe Whipple could wake up fast if he had to, action was his maiden name you might say, and all he said was "Oh lordy, lordy," and then while he was still buttoning his pants, he was loping over to Aunt Thea's place and pounding on *her* door, and Rolf was just waking up and thinking *he* had barely got to sleep. Here's what had happened:

It was a busted rail that wrecked the Q, near a siding called View Point, although there wasn't nothing to view there. A few miles away they had a section house, and an Irish foreman by the name of James Hegan, and some shanties for his help. Hegan's brother worked for him, by the name of Bill, and they was both married to Indian girls, and was related to most of the rest of the gang.

So James Hegan sent Bill out to stand watch on the train that night, and one brakie, an Irishman by the name of Pat Dunne, stayed too. Long before daylight, James took the pump car and a push car and all thirteen of his Indian hands out to start getting ready for the wrecker.

Not a care in the world. There wasn't no reason to leave a guard there, nobody was going to steal a wrecked train was there, and the only reason was to give his brother Bill a night away from his wife, who was in one of her mean streaks. The only reason Pat Dunne stayed, he was lame in the back from having got throwed off'n a car in the wreck, and it would be easier than riding back into town on a hand car, and then coming out again.

No sir, not a care in the world! Yet when they got there, Bill Hegan and Pat Dunne was both dead. Bill had been shot twice in the back, so prob'ly whoever it was sneaked up on him, but Pat Dunne had tried to run away, lame back and all, and had been finely cornered and shot in the top of the head with a .45, prob'ly, like he'd been on his knees begging for mercy.

"Rolf, these ain't no gang of chicken stealers going around and lifting a fry off'n somebody's roost, no they ain't; I got some murdering sons of bitches here, and I've got to raise a posse and go after them," Abe said.

Rolf said wait, he'd go with him, but Abe said, "No, Father Lavrens ought to be down around Dalton somewhere, that's a place southeast of here used to be a stage station but it's dying now, but he's got a few stray Catholics there, and he stops in and combs and brushes their faith now and then. Both of these dead men was Irish, so they'll be his to bury, unless the railroad decides it's less trouble to haul them to Denver. I don't want that old Norwegian priest on my tail. I'll take the blame, it happened in my jurisdiction, but I wish you could find a way to urge him to ask the Lord to temper the wind to the shorn lamb, because I'm clipped close to the hide this time," Abe said.

He rode off with his *posse comitatus,* the usual bunch of loafers, and Rolf saddled up and took off down the Dalton trail. In a little while he seen the priest coming towards him on a big old horse almost as old as he was, and Father Lavrens was seventy-seven then, a big old red-faced Norwegian. He never had much use for the other Protestant preachers that came and went around Mooney, but he took a liking to Rolf right away. Partly it was because Rolf was half Swede, although at other times Father Lavrens said a Swede was only a Norwegian with his brains knocked out.

Father Lavrens's horse wouldn't stir out of a walk, and he didn't want it to. He said, "Abe's up against it, I'm afraid, and it's too bad because we're sure to get worse. The scum always floats to the top if you roil the waters enough."

Rolf said, "He'll be relieved to know you feel this way. You've been a powerful worry to him."

"Because of this Sephardic Jewish nonsense? Or it may not be nonsense, we're all God's family, only some of us behave better than others, as in any family," the priest said.

"That goes for even Methodists?" Rolf said.

"Even Methodists. You're willful and blind and stubborn, you're undutiful children of a loving Father, and you flee from the affectionate discipline of the one true Church, but I've been commanded to love you and I try to be an obedient son. Which I don't think is true of yourself, since you served a prison term," the priest answered him.

"I don't know as that's a fair statement. I was unjustly convicted and I got pardoned out," Rolf said.

They sloshed that argument around some, and then Rolf found himself telling the priest about that business in the hammock, although he hadn't intended to, because ordinarily it was the kind of thing any man would keep to himself, especially somebody like Rolf.

"I haven't a doubt that it was God you heard," Father Lavrens said. "Keep listening for it, and I'm just as sure that someday you'll hear from Him again, and He'll tell you to go the rest of the way, and unite with the one true church."

"I doubt that," Rolf said, "and I couldn't cut it if He did. I hope you won't take it the wrong way, but somehow I can't swallow the pope."

"Why not?" Father Lavrens said.

Rolf tried to explain, how Jesus went around with the worst hard-up riffraff in town, and had to mooch His grub and a place to stay, and He told them to give all they had to the poor and follow Him, and so on. And here the pope was on a golden throne, wearing golden robes, and you had to kneel down and lick his hand, and Pontius Pilate and Herod both never had it as rich.

"Never forget, young man, that the pope is a man," Father

Lavrens said, "as every pope before him has been a man, and as priests always have been, still are, and always will be men. Don't ask that we perform the miracles necessary to revive the simple creed of Jesus Christ. The miracle is that in a world of thrones and kings and empires, of wars and rebellions, of wholesale murder and the desolation of nations, the Holy Church has survived at all. When power was used to exterminate us, we asked God for power to help us survive, and He gave it to us. We erected our own throne, and made the heir of St. Peter as glorious as the richest and most ignorant king. We showed the Holy Father reverence, clothing him in golden robes and kissing his hand, to demonstrate to jealous kings that we were ready to die for our pope, our church, and our God, though every jealous king in the world threw his armies against us. Yet all this time, beneath the robes of the pope was the student of the simple fisherman he succeeded, do you see that?"

"In a way," Rolf said.

Father Lavrens smiled. "But in a way no, is that it? The time is coming when it will be no longer necessary to impress kings and emperors—when mankind will have progressed to the point where we can again live in peace and trust and brotherhood, and a simple fisherman can again lead us. I don't expect to live to see those times, but they can't be far off, say the turn of the century, yes sir about 1900 the last throne should have toppled, don't you think?"

"I couldn't say," Rolf said.

Father Lavrens said, "I look forward to that, young man. Imperfect republics take their places, but they're still republics because man is better than he used to be, thanks to the mercy of God, and he will be better still. Change comes faster and faster! Prophecy can now be carried over the electric telegraph wire, think of that! So can sin, you will say, but sin has always been a fast traveler, and still the truth outruns it because it has what a cowboy calls 'bottom.' You know how, when his horse founders in a race, the cowboy says he 'bottoms out,' well, the truth of God never bottoms out! No, I won't see God's golden age, but you will, when the pope will step down off his throne at last, and the love and peace and brotherhood of the golden age will have arrived, and there will be no rich and no poor, no strong and no weak, only the children of God. And when that happens, young man, remember that it was an ignorant old cow-country priest who told you so, in his seventy-eighth year."

He could really talk when he got wound up, but he was talking to a man who had did time in the pen, and it seemed to Rolf that he knowed more about miserable human nature than Father Lavrens did, and the golden age was a good deal further off than he thought. Another thousand years was more like it, as these two murders at the Q would kind of demonstrate.

Father Lavrens was played out when he got to Mooney. He said any ride of more than a couple of miles was getting too much for him, he felt fine except for a little prostate trouble, but he didn't have the strength he had fifty years ago. Rolf helped him into his shack behind Blessed Sacrament, which wasn't more than a shack itself, and brought him a pail of fresh water, and picked some cucumbers for him from the vine by his back door, and took care of his horse. Cucumbers was all he needed, having priested a hitch in the desert, where they're raised for both food and drink.

"Find out where the bodies are going, if you can," Father Lavrens said. "If they're to be buried here, I'll have to get my strength back."

"I'll do the best I can," Rolf said. "I'd bury them for you if I could, but I reckon I couldn't, and they didn't live long enough for me to hear their dying confession and grant absolution, so it's past the point where a mere Protestant can do any good."

The priest said, "What do you mean, hear their confessions and grant absolution? You're uttering a grave impiety young man, this verges on sacrilege." Rolf told him what he had got from the chaplain, and they argued about it awhile, and the priest said that at best it would be a pretty makeshift sort of unction, and the Protestant that dared to tackle it had better be in a high state of grace himself. He said he'd look into it when he could get to his books again, and he hadn't had time to read much in the last twenty or twenty-five years, and maybe he had slipped up on something, but he said, "I would hate to rely on you to grant peace to my own sinful soul, for example. I want something other than a cowboy hearing my last confession!"

Rolf said he didn't blame him, most cowboys was pretty ignorant, and then Father Lavrens complained that his feet burned, so Rolf got a gourd of water and washed them for him. He asked him if he didn't have no clean socks, and Father Lavrens said he didn't think so, when summer came he usually turned his feet out to grass in sandals, but he hadn't got any sandals yet. So Rolf washed out his socks for him too, and hung them up in the sun to dry, and a mighty wore-out pair they was, too.

So then Rolf got his nerve up, and asked Father Lavrens if he could get his advice on something that didn't have nothing to do with religion or the church, just an idee of his own, a hunch that bothered him. A priest gets used to giving out the advice he's hired to give, so there's nothing in it for him any more except getting impatient with the same old cussedness he hears all the time. But you ask him for some man-to-man advice, nothing professional, and you've got yourself an interested priest, and Father Lavrens was.

Rolf told him about this secret hunch that was bothering him, and he said, "I'm taking a lot for granted. I'm putting my own judgment up against the whole county, including Abe Whipple."

Father Lavrens said, "Let me ask you this—how strongly do you believe in what you call your hunch? Do you have an overwhelming conviction in your heart as well as your mind, that it is this way and no other?"

"I sure don't," Rolf said. "If I felt that way, why would I need advice?"

"If you had given me any other answer," the priest said, "I

would have told you, 'Shoo, boy, forget it, don't bother me!'
But I'm afraid to say it's your prison-wise knowledge of mortal
man, which I envy you not at all, that bares the truth to you."

"But suppose I take a chance, and I'm still wrong?" Rolf
wanted to know.

"Why then you'll be sincerely wrong, and I trust sincerely
penitent for it. Now let me sleep. You can be a pest, you know,
burdened with a conscience almost as heavy as your igno-
rance. Shoo, boy, shoo!" Father Lavrens said.

Rolf got on his bony old horse and headed back into Mooney,
and this was the very minute that the old Zimmerman house
fell in, the oldest house in town, and always a lot of talk about
saving it as a historical relic, it being the town's first post office,
and some people had been murdered there, and the first twins
in Colorado born there, one on the way to the bed and one in
the bed. But people kept talking about preserving it, and the
house kept getting older, and the last Zimmerman was living
in Denver and wanted two hundred dollars for it, and nobody could make up his mind to put in some of his own money
to start the pot going.

It was an old log house with a fireplace, and it had had a
roof of hand-split cedar shakes, but most of the shakes was
gone, and the old pole rafters leaned every which way, and
the town milk cows scratching against the corners had weak-
ened the joints. There was five boys in her when she went
down, the pole rafters going first, knocking each other over like
dominoes, and then the long west wall, and then the short
south wall with the fireplace. The fireplace stood though, in silent tribute to whoever built it. A lot of people wondered what
them boys was doing in there, the general opinion being some
kind of nastiness, and they was prob'ly right. But most of the
grown men in Mooney could remember being in there as kids,
and she didn't cave in on them. So there wasn't as much talk
about the hand of God as you might expect, because none of
the boys was killed, or even hurt, and when people talk about
the hand of God, what they usually mean is some kind of death
and disaster.

15

Abe was back so soon it was clear he had rode hard both ways. His posse was worth the price of the ride, and no more, and his deputy had disappeared into a honeymoon fog, and Abe was so stumped he had kind of a horrified expression. He said they had took the remains of Bill Hegan and Pat Dunne on to Denver, so Father Lavrens could forget about that.

But the extra train had come in with the wrecker, and it had thirty-three Irishmen on it and eighteen Italians, a total of fifty-one tough young bucks, each fresh from his own Old Country, and still smelling of the immigration louse powder. They had been roughed up somewhat on the long trip, and was as spooky as brush calves when they was finely dumped out on the free arid soil of Colorado. And then the first thing they heard about was the murder of two fellow Catholics, because any time you find an Irishman or an Italian who is not a Catholic, it's like a double-yolk egg for scarce.

Their families had prob'ly warned them against this country, saying they'd either have to join the Protestants or be gelded, and then the Q expected them to horse that train up without a meal, until the cook in the kitchen car sobered up enough to fry some eggs or beans or something. There could of been real trouble if Abe hadn't of showed up then, but he went out there without his guns on, and offered to take them foreigners on two at a time if they'd wait their turns, and fight the fair American way, anything went except knives.

You tell an immigrant Irishman or Italian to fall in like a soldier, and call him a son of a bitch, and offer to whip him two at a time, and one of two things is going to happen, either you've got to make good or he's going to love you. These boys was hungry for a familiar word, and they throwed down their pick handles and told Abe their troubles, and he could understand enough of the Irish brogue to get it straight. He turned the cook out of bed, and put him on the end of his rope, and led him at a nice steady trot in his underwear for a mile or two, and he decided he was in shape to wallop a pot or two after all.

"Just when I think we've got peace on earth," Abe said, "this is when they discover somebody has robbed the Goddamn train, prob'ly the same miscreants that killed them two men, because who else had the chance? Rolf, you can't have no idee what they got away with! There was three bales of Chinese silk worth six hundred dollars each, and ten cases of good whisky, and a crate of twenty-four rifles with twelve thousand rounds of ammunition, and five cases of dynamite, and a gross of primers, and two cases of paregoric in pint bottles, and a gross of butcher knives. The rifles and ammunition and dynamite, they're bad enough, but with good whisky selling for eighty cents a quart, it's that paregoric that upsets me. You take an Indian, and sell him whisky made of water and caramel syrup and paregoric, and you've got an Indian who's going to wake up and go on the warpath, and you arm him with some of them old cheap butcher knives, somebody's going to have to kill the poor son of a bitch before he hurts somebody. Rolf, this is the most fiendish thing I ever seen! That stuff went out of there on a wagon, we know that, it had to, but it rained like hell up there just before daylight, and there ain't no more tracks than on a brick road."

"Yes, what I wanted to—" Rolf tried to say.

Abe hit a tree with his fist, and skinned his fist a little, and the tree too, and busted in, "And that train was deliberately and fiendishly wrecked. Some bold son of a bitch dug out from under three or four ties about four feet from a rail joint, and then he chiseled the angle-bar bolts of the joint off, and that took some time. He couldn't expect that rail was going to break and part of it turn over, but it did, so he had himself not just a simple derailment, but a first-class wreck. Now here's something else that puzzles me; this has to be the work of a gang, no one man or even two is going to pull a job like *this'n*, but the signs show that when them big heavy bales of silk was loaded, they was pinched along a little at a time by pinch bars. Now that's a lot of trouble to go to, and what are they going to do with it now they got it? You can't just load nearly a thousand pounds of Chinese silk up in your saddlebags, and go around peddling it to various women. Rolf, this thing is creepy! It's like a crow picking up pieces of glass and tin to hide in his nest, there's no sense in it, but no harm either except to waste his time, and what's time to a crow? But these ain't crows, and I put it to anybody, if he's got a plan to dispose of three bales of Chinese silk, then this is the same miscreant son of a bitch that run off with Cal Venaman's steers last winter. *That* wasn't no home-town pilferage either!"

Rolf caught him temporarily breathless, and he said, "Rest your mind and your mouth a minute, Abe, and tell me one thing if you can. What kind of a winter did Jack Butler have last winter?"

"The usual kind, drunk. I don't know why you plague me with the problems of a common sot at a time like this, but I know that during them January blizzards, there was twice the ignorant son of a bitch would of froze to death if some of the Flying V boys hadn't come along and pried him out of a snowbank. Why do you bother me with a common drunk at a time like this?"

"Because," Rolf said, "I don't think he's a common drunk, is why."

Abe didn't say nothing, but he knowed Rolf wasn't a word waster, not out of the pulpit anyway, but he come to a point like a bird dog. Rolf said, "Abe, I took a quart of whisky out to the ranch with us last time, to break Jack of his habit or drownd him. When I seen a fit coming on him, I took him down and poured it down him like drenching a sick horse. How much do you think it would take to get that man drunk?"

"Why," said Abe, "if you only had a quart, you'd only have a starter."

"A half pint done it," Rolf said.

"*What?*" Abe said.

Rolf said, "From the first, he was just too pitiful a sot to me, Abe, every cent he had ought to of gone into his thirst, but he's got a nice tight cabin with even scrim curtains, and fences like he was raising race horses, and bobwire enough to put a fence around the county, and a dresser full of nice new clothes he never wore. You never seen a good whisky sot that et very much, but Jack is a pure hog for his grub, you couldn't bake enough light bread to fill him, and he wants butter on it too, and bacon boiled in his beans, and anything you bring home to eat, he'll eat it. Now look here—he was passed out drunk when Colonel Pegler T. Saymill was murdered, and was beyond suspicion. He was passed out drunk when Cal Venaman's house was robbed and his dogs killed, and was beyond suspicion. And I can testify personally that he was passed out drunk when that train was wrecked and them men killed, or at least he had that excuse, because I personally poured half a pint down him. Then he went out for a long hard punishing ride to sober up, and I'll tell you this, he looked punished all right when he got back. *But he left most of that whisky in the bottle, Abe.* What I think, this man can't drink at all!"

Abe shook his head. "Only listen here, Rolf; I trailed them critters of Cal's as fur as Keith County, Nebraska, last winter. I talked to two men that said they heard they was sold for eight dollars each to somebody that paid cash, and then drove them north by east, and there wasn't a couple of hundred like Cal thinks, there was three hundred and two of his steers. Cal would hang himself if he knowed that, and you can't blame him, but you can't blame Jack Butler either.

"Because we're talking about $2,416 worth of cash steers, and $1,600 in gold from the house robbery, and $600 from Peg Saymill, and Jack Butler is a man that bets one-cent chips in two-cent raises, what the hell is he going to do with three bales of Chinese silk, and all that other stuff? Jack Butler is just *nobody,* he couldn't talk nobody into being his gang, why any robber worth his salt would laugh himself sick at the idee of being part of Jack Butler's gang!"

Rolf said, "Abe, in prison we had a little old nobody fella too, nobody took him serious either, so he'd go around and make a mysterious sign on things, a circle with a line drawed through it was all. It didn't mean a thing, but we felt sorry for the poor booger, and we didn't want him to feel neglected and slip a knife into somebody, so we took it serious. Like we'd all shiver when he was around, and say my goodness what does this mysterious sign mean, scratched on the wall in the can, and in the dust on the surgery table in the hospital, what are we coming to? It made this poor ignorant convict as happy as if he had good sense.

"This is the kind of robber Jack was, a plain old scrabbling two-bit cowman, but in his mind he's simply next to God. Killing don't mean a thing to him; behind that face he's laughing himself sick at us because he knows who done these killings and we don't, and he'll do some more if he ain't catched. The prisons is full of men that think they're too good for the rest of us. They don't need a woman, they don't need money, they don't need a dog or a cat, or even a prison rat that can be trained to come back for some crumbs. All they need is just to know that, in secret, they're smarter and better than everybody else in the county.

"There's just one thing wrong with the whole idee, Abe. Brains! Jack Butler couldn't plan how to empty a bootful of you know what, he'd cut a hole in the toe first; he could drive a four-horse team to a wagon, if somebody supplied the horses and wagon, or he could do the killing, or use a pinch bar to load three bales of Chinese silk. But he ain't got the brains to lay out the plans for this, he's hardly got any brains at all, he can't even make a convincing drunk!"

Abe kept nodding and sighing, and nodding and sighing, and then he said, "What gravels me, Rolf, is Jack ain't the only ranny that thinks he's smarter than us, there's another one just like him only worse, and the hell of it is, he *is!* Well, man may toil from sun to sun, but a sheriff's work is never done, as the poet says. I'd like to contribute one more thought before we have the closing ceremonials, I'll enjoy arresting this twitchy little son of a bitch more than I do most arrests."

"Don't go off half-cocked on my surmises, Abe," Rolf said. "I been wrong in my time, you know."

"You ain't wrong about this. This has stared me in the face for months, only I never spent two years in the pen to learn the sad truth about my fellow man, that the son of a bitch is even more unreliable than he looks," Abe said.

He went out of there calm as a cucumber, and Rolf could only hope he didn't walk into an ambush in that cold but angry frame of mind. Forty minutes later he was back, empty-handed. He set down and took off his hat and shook his head like he was getting rid of a buzzing in his ears, and maybe he was. He said:

"Rolf, ever notice that big bay gelding in the back box stall at the livery barn in Lickety Split? Well you missed a horse, son! Well that horse belonged to Huey Haffener, and Tattooed Emily, his Number One girl, told me he rode out on that horse last evening and ain't been seen since. He dug up the floor of the cellar, so he prob'ly took his valuables with him, and he even borried money off'n some of the girls before he left. A total of $144 he beat them poor hard-working girls out of, can you beat that?

"Rolf, I'm whipped, and I deserve it. I might just as well hand this star to some six-year-old girl for all the good I am. But I'll have to say this in behalf of myself, if Thad Rust turns out to be worth two whoops in hell on this job, it'll be because of what I learned him, not any native talent, because native talent is one thing he hasn't got, unless it's one he's keeping employed right now. He's your next sheriff sure as hell!"

Rolf said, "Don't give up yet, Abe. Lend me a good horse, and you just keep the eggs warm on the nest until you hear from me again."

"You can have any horse of mine any time, you know that," Abe said, "but you little piss-ant you, what are you up to? You're a minister of the gospel, like it or not! You've put your hand to the plow, and you can't turn back just because an old wooden-head sheriff overstayed his time on the job."

Rolf said, "I ain't taking no chances of no kind, Abe. I'm just doing what I knowed had to be done a long time ago, and would of been done if I hadn't got sidetracked on this preaching foolishness."

This was when he come to see me. I'd been looking for it for a right smart, and when I heard the dogs, I got up and went out, and there he was on one of Abe Whipple's horses.

First thing I noticed was how middle-aged and steady he looked, not like the wild old nothing kind of a kid he used to be. He seen I didn't have no gun on, and I seen he didn't have one, so he pulled in his horse and just waited, but I figgered it was his move to speak.

So he said, "Hello there, Holbrook."

I said, "Howdy, Rolf, but I don't go under the name of Holbrook Cohelan no more. I'm Peter S. Heath, Pete Heath, around here."

He said, "I know that. Mr. Heath, you owe me one."

I said how did he figger that. He said, "Well, partly the Red, White, and Blue deal but mostly the Missouri Pacific, and if that wasn't the most ignorant kind of a robbery, it'll do till one comes along."

I had these two dogs, a mostly mastiff bitch by the name of Spot, and one of her pups that I called Foolish, and as long as you was on horseback with them you was all right, but get down on the ground and see what happened. I had to tie them in the dugout where I stored my spuds, and then Rolf got down and we went into my place. I had this little old shanty down near the Platte, in the homestead country, called Pete Heath's Place, where you could buy groceries and tobacco and so forth, and ammunition, and I run a little game there. I never set in myself, only took a penny out of every dollar in the pot, and there wasn't a crooked dealer anywhere that dared set in there. I knowed them all.

Rolf didn't offer to shake hands, but he set down and said, "You're looking mighty fit for a man carrying so much metal in him."

I said, "Well, I have a lot of pain, and a regret or two, but mostly I'm satisfied with life. So you are a minister of the gospel now."

He said, "Not for long. I've got to ask you for something, Pete Heath, and I'm going to overlook the Missouri Pacific proposition entirely, and just say three words to you, Red, White, and Blue."

This went back to when him and me went up into the Black Hills. We worked first in a gold mine, but you take a cowboy that has always earned his dollar a day on a horse, mucking in a mine is a low-down way to earn an extra four bits, so we quit in disgust. There was this Red, White, and Blue saloon there, run by a fella by the name of John Hamilton Shaefer, that had been a captain in the cavalry, but had to resign when he was caught raping a squaw. If she had been an officer's squaw he could of been in bad trouble, but he was only a sergeant, Sergeant Backsy, so there was only an inquiry by the colonel, and John Hamilton Shaefer got the choice of resigning or taking a court martial for conduct unbecoming.

When he said he'd resign, Sergeant Backsy got up and said what the hell kind of justice was this, he'd kiss your foot if this was justice, so they busted him back to private and give him ten days in the stockade. John Hamilton Shaefer started this gambling hell called the Red, White, and Blue, the rawest games you ever seen. So when Rolf and me went broke, we decided to relieve Mr. Shaefer of some of his ill-gotten gains, so we went in the morning about 4 A.M., and put our guns on him, and took what gold there was in the strongbox, about $110. Only when we took out the back way, Mr. Shaefer ups with a damn little old .25 caliber derringer and shot me in the intestines, and I dropped the gold, and only had time to pick

up four ten-dollar pieces, less than Rolf and me had lost in his
dirty crooked games.

With that little slug in my intestines, I could of died if Rolf
hadn't took care of me, so I owed him one for that all right.
He wanted to know where Huey Haffener and Jack Butler
would be headed with their loot. I didn't know about the train
being robbed, only about the wreck, so it was shocking news
to me.

I said, "So they're finely out in the open. It was a pure mar-
vel how long they got away with it. I'll tell you what I can,
Rolf. There's a freighter in Cheyenne, Louie Isbel, that runs
a freight line. He got in over his head for some fancy imported
horses, and it was him that brought a couple of men down to
help Jack move them Flying V cattle they stole, and he said
they just froze their hind ends off for less than fifty dollars
apiece. Now you tell me there's three bales of Chinese silk
and quite a bit of other heavy stuff, now that spells Louie Isbel
to me, because he can move it and warehouse it until Huey
finds somebody to buy it. There's a little old grassy canyon
where Louie Isbel will hole up, and rest his horses, and wait
for the fuss to die down, and he hasn't got any more guts than
Huey or Jack. All Abe has to do is go in shooting, and he's got
them."

He said this was what he wanted to know, and how could
he find this canyon. I tried to tell him how, but he didn't know
the country up there, and he said he'd have to have a map to
give Abe. I said no sir, I was through with crime, but now and
then somebody came through that wasn't, and I didn't want
none of my handwriting on anything to put me in a bad position.

He said he'd make the map if I'd tell him how, and we
rustled around and couldn't find a single piece of paper anywhere, and neither of us had the habit of carrying paper on
us. I had this piece of slate I had quarried from the creek bed,
with a three-corner chip of it for a slate pencil, and he drawed
the map according to my directions.

He got up on the sheriff's horse, and I handed him up the

piece of slate, about a foot and a half square, and he said, "I told you I'd call it square between us, and I will, Holbrook, or rather Pete. But I come into this country to kill you for letting me go to prison on that Missouri Pacific deal, and it still rankles. It ain't easy to give up two years of your life that way."

I said, "I bet it ain't, but sometimes one man draws the Queen of Spades, and sometimes the other'n. I just wonder how you can have the guts to remind me of the Red, White, and Blue, after you played me false on the Missouri Pacific proposition."

He said, "Me played you false? How do you figger I played you false?"

I said, "There's no profit in digging up the dead, but by God I wouldn't of went into that with no such fool as Bobby Dale if you hadn't gone into it! Here I am a fugitive with a price on my head, and you're in prison it's true, but if you didn't light on your feet I'd like to know who did, assistant to the chaplain! I heard you was down on me because of the Missouri Pacific job, and I wasn't surprised because you always did have a short temper, but by God I got deadfalled into that one, and I wasn't going to shoot it out with you! No sir, I would of plugged you from behind with a rifle the minute you showed up here!"

He said why didn't I, and I said I'd heard he was preaching in the church in Mooney, and it was just like that unpredictable son of a bitch, and let's see how long it lasts. I said, "Rolf, you was the best sidekick I ever had, but don't throw up that Missouri Pacific proposition to me, because you're set for life with one of the easiest jobs in the world, and I'm scratching a living the meanest kind of way. I ain't one to complain that life ain't fair, or you'd sure hear me complaining now!"

He said, "Mr. Heath, I swear to you I never knowed Bobby Dale in my life, and I never knowed anything about that Missouri Pacific robbery until I was arrested for it, and I don't have no idee how you possibly figgered I could be in on something as foolish as that."

I seen it all then, this Bobby Dale had lied to me to get me to go in with him; there couldn't be no other explanation because Bobby Dale would lie to his own mother, and I never knowed Rolf Ledger to lie to anybody. We shook hands, and I felt mighty good about that, and I reckon he did too, because he said, "The hardest thing in the world is to believe that a friend has let you down, and that's what I've had to believe all these years."

I said me too, and we shook hands again, and I said maybe someday I'd get up early enough to come in and listen to him preach. He said it would prob'ly do me good to listen to anybody, but he was giving it up.

I said if he was giving it up, I reckoned I never would get started on it, and he said religion would do me good and bring me peace of mind. I said, "I already got peace of mind, it's a hardscrabble way for an old cowboy to live, but I brung it on myself and I know it. Religion is a cash proposition, and I can't afford it. Prob'ly Jesus meant well, but if there's been a clergyman since then that wasn't out for the dollar, history has overlooked him. It's like a bunch of these new mail-order stores, all fighting over the same business. The pope has got one store, and the archbishop of Canterbury has got one, and there's a couple of other pretty big ones, and a regular epidemic of little crossroads bargain places dealing mostly in secondhand goods. Whenever they scrape the trade dry between them, they load up a nice stock of piety and go over to Africa and pester the cannibals, and all *they* want is to be let alone the same as me. I'd love to hear you preach once, though, Rolf Ledger, just to see the spectacle. I bet you ten dollars you couldn't get up there in the pulpit and look me in the eye."

He said, "You'd lose that bet, Mr. Heath," and he turned his horse around, and I let Spot and Foolish out, and hoped nobody would ever find out it was me that told on Louie Isbel. Not that I owed him anything, but it's a matter of principle.

16

Rolf had his doubts about that map, but Abe just said, "Oh yes, I know the area well, and it seems I've seen this piece of slate before too."

"It's pretty common around here," Rolf said.

"Yes," said Abe, "but this is an uncommon good piece. I hope you didn't go to a lot of trouble getting it."

Rolf knowed what he meant, and he said, "I didn't. A nice profit for both parties."

Abe said, "I watched that Peter S. Heath for quite a while, let me tell you, until in my judgment I decided he was keeping his tugs tight and his crupper buckled, so I let him be. Some sheriffs might of rode him clear out of the county, but I didn't, and here's the bread I cast on the water coming back to me. So we'll just rub it out, and there you are, a nice clean slate again."

He spit on the slate and rubbed the map out, and put some more .45 shells in his belts, and throwed his saddle on another horse. Rolf said he was going with him, and Abe said, "No you ain't. I'm only grateful I haven't got Thad Rust to handicap me, a man of the cloth would be more than I could stand. Thad never was much help, and he'll be a month getting over his backache and catching up on his sleep; no thank you, Reverend, I've got problems enough without you along."

He picked Bill Ahern and Alf Constable and Johnny Wyatt, a nephew of Rachel and cousin to poor old eager Lettie, all good steady men, good shots, and used to his highhanded way of doing things. Not every man could ride to Abe's orders.

It was almost dark when they left town, and they went a roundabout way in case anybody was keeping watch for Huey, which wasn't likely. Abe told his men, "Huey won't be no trouble. Staying alive is always his main concern. But this fool of a Jack Butler prob'ly imagines he's some kind of a damn tornado of a badman, and he'll draw his weapon. Let's don't stain our souls with killing that deluded riffraff. Let's save him to hang."

"What I want to know," Bill Ahern said, "is where we're going."

"You'll find out," Abe said. "Discipline, that's what puts steel into an attack! Learn to do as you're told without a lot of questions, and you'll be steady on the firing line. Just notice where my suspenders cross, and keep that between your horse's ears, and you'll get to the right place at the right time."

"Your rump is a lot easier to follow, nobody could miss that," Johnny Wyatt said.

They got up on the Flying V range, and Abe told them to lay down and catch a little sleep, he'd watch the horses, and so they did. He booted them out a while later, and kept them amused by quarreling with them until almost daylight, when they come to where these fugitives was holed up.

They had to admire the place all right, plenty of feed for the teams, and a nice spring of sweet water, and in grass so deep the tracks wouldn't last long for anybody to foller. As near as anybody could remember, the spring was a good half mile up from where they had to stop, around a bend.

"Now let's see, here's how we'll do this," Abe said. "You all wait here. I'll dismount and go around them afoot, and see what we're up against."

Bill Ahern said, "You old fat aged fool, it'll be noon before you get anywhere afoot. I'll go see myself what we're up against."

Abe said well all right, but use his head for a change. Abe and Alf and Johnny stood down and held their horses and

Bill's, and Bill sauntered off through the grass until he had to get down on his hands and knees, and that was the last they seen of him for a while, and all they could do was stand there and slap mosquitoes and make sure the horses didn't make any noise.

Bill got up on the rise, and he could see the camp of the desperadoes, and them four big beautiful draft horses just catched his breath, they was so beautiful. Four matched Clydesdales, two browns and two chestnuts that would average nineteen hundred pounds each in working flesh. The wagon was turned around already, so they wouldn't have to fool around turning it when they got ready to move out. There was only one other horse Bill could see, Huey Haffener's big bay.

Huey was setting on his knees beside the wagon, with his derby hat on and a cigar in his mouth, and it looked to Bill like he was counting his money. There wasn't no sign of Jack Butler or this Cheyenne freighter Louie Isbel, but Bill figgered they'd be around somewhere, because Huey couldn't even harness one of them Clydesdales, let alone drive a four-horse hitch of them.

Bill got down on his hands and knees and started around them. There wasn't no trees nowhere, but about a hundred yards from the camp there was this spring, with a lot of brush around it, the nearest thing to cover in miles. Bill got there, and had a nice drink of fresh water, and made himself a cigarette, because he didn't figger Huey would notice if he was to fly a kite.

In a few minutes, Jack Butler crawled out from under the wagon, rubbing his eyes and yawning. Bill threw his cigarette into the mud and squatted there listening. He could hear every word they said.

Huey said, "Morning, Jack, did you sleep well?"

Jack said, "No thanks to you if I did."

"Cheer up, Jack! We got the world by the tail with a down-hill pull," Huey said.

"Maybe you have, but I left a ten-thousand-dollar property

back there and I never can go back, the prettiest little property in the world," Jack said.

"You stupid son of a bitch, you owed so much on that property, you couldn't of sold out for six hundred net," Huey said.

"I had more than that in bobwire," Jack said.

"The more fool you! Man that can't handle money, he don't deserve it. But that's behind us. I was just computing; you've got eight hundred and forty dollars coming right now, more money than you ever had in your life," Huey come back.

"I had more than that from Cal Venaman's house. I took all the chances, and like a fool I just handed that money over to you," Jack kind of whimpered.

"Fair is fair. I was the one told you the money was there, wasn't I?" said Huey.

"You never do anything except *tell*. Somebody else has to take the chances. Where the hell is Louie?" Jack said.

"You know where he is, Cheyenne, to find us a place to hide this stuff. You can't just go driving into Cheyenne and start looking for a place in broad daylight. Don't try to think, Jack. That's where you get into trouble every time, when you try to think. Get us some breakfast and feed these horses of Louie's, and let me do the thinking," Huey said.

"Why did he have to ride my horse? That Fanny mare is the only thing I got left from the days when I was a cattleman on my own J Bar B property," Jack complained.

"He had to ride something, and I don't allow strangers on my horse, you know that, Jack," Huey said.

Jack said he had to have a drink of water, so he come down to the spring and got down on his hands and knees and leaned over, kind of complaining to himself about how he was doing all the work and what was he getting out of it, sore hands was all. Bill got up and leaned down and hit him in the back of the neck, and then fished him out of the spring before he could drownd, and then hit him again to make sure he stayed asleep.

Nothing looks sillier than a city fella trying to get by on the prairie. It don't matter how shrewd he is, setting in his own saloon in his checked pants and deerskin vest, surrounded by beautiful fallen women and drinking them rotgut French wines, he's just an orphan calf if you get him out in the prairie. Bill dragged Jack a ways by the ankle, and then he started to come to, and Bill had to wallop him again, and then he got up and throwed him across his shoulder, and Huey never did even suspicion how close he was.

"Well well, so here is one of our miscreants," Abe said, when Bill carried Jack up over his shoulder. "I judge he didn't give you no trouble. What are the other two doing?"

Bill said that Huey was counting his money, and Louie Isbel was gone to Cheyenne on Jack's Fanny mare, and they might as well forget him for a couple of days. "You ought to see them beautiful Clydesdale horses, Abe," Bill said. "Somebody's going to get them horses. I want you to help me figger out a way to bid them in."

"You don't want Clydesdales in this country," Abe said. "A Clydesdale will eat as much as an army remount, that horse has got to be grain fed, that's not a horse for the frontier, you don't want Clydesdales."

Bill said he reckoned he knowed what he wanted, and Abe said Bill might as well drink his money up as pour it down a Clydesdale's throat in oats and rolled barley, and so on. They tied Jack's hands behind him good and tight, and left him lay there sound asleep. They didn't tie his feet, because he wasn't going no place anyway, and it might be fun if he tried to.

They went down and gathered Huey in without much trouble, although he was expecting Jack Butler and lost his head when he looked up instead and seen the sheriff and a posse, and he yanked out a pocket gun and tried to shoot. Abe slapped him across the mouth for that, and made him drop the gun, and that took all the fight out of him. He had put his money away in a tin box that he had kept buried in the floor of his cellar in the Jackrabbit, and they took the key away from him and opened it up and counted out $15,980 in gold pieces.

"That money is mine, nobody lays a hand on that money, it's mine, leave my money alone," Huey kept saying, until they had to slap him again. They tied his hands behind him too, and Bill hitched up them four Clydesdales, calling them darling and sweetheart and so on while he done it. He asked Huey what their names was, and Huey said the leaders was Betty and Candy, and the wheelers was Dolly and Bonny, but Bill went on calling them darling and sweetheart. They walked out of there with that big heavy overloaded wagon like they was dragging a piece of grocery-store string behind them, with Huey tied on behind on a ten-foot leash, so he had to trot to keep up.

Abe and Johnny and Alf rode ahead, and the first thing they noticed was that Jack Butler wasn't nowhere in sight, and Abe said he wondered where the fool had went to, and just then a rifle bullet plunked into Johnny Wyatt in the side. He fell off'n his horse, and the others jumped off'n theirs, and just in time too, because here come another rifle bullet that didn't miss Abe by more than an inch or two.

Abe hollered back for Bill not to come no closer, some son of a bitch was shooting at them. He asked Johnny how he was, and Johnny said, "Why I'm shot, how the hell do you think I am? You led me out here on a wild-goose chase and got me shot."

Abe had him pull his shirttail out so he could look at the hole, and he said, "It's not the worst I ever seen, Johnny, but I can well believe it stings, so you take it easy and the rest of us will handle things from here on out."

"Small comfort to me," Johnny said.

They had let the horses run, and that's what they done, they run. Abe said, "Bet you a nickel this Louie Isbel didn't go to Cheyenne after all, because nobody but a fool teamster would let a man get down in deep grass where he had to hunt him out. Let's kind of fan out, everybody stay low to the ground, and let him come after us. This could take quite a while now, boys, so don't get impatient, remember how the Indians did it; that's the game, boys, we play it like Indians."

They spread out and stayed hid in the grass, and pretty soon they seen this fella on Jack Butler's mare Fanny, setting up there with a rifle in his hand and the butt on his hip. He knowed he was safe, because he had got a good look at them, and he knowed none of them had rifles.

There wasn't no sign of Jack Butler, but they knowed Jack wouldn't be far away. They knowed this fella had come back and found Jack and turned him loose, and knowed how things stood, the camp captured by now, and the four Clydesdales and the wagon in the hands of the law.

This fella hollered, "Sheriff, hey, Sheriff!" Abe just set there in the grass and sucked on a piece of grass, and didn't pay no more attention than if somebody else had been sheriff.

This fella hollered again, "Sheriff, I'll make you a deal. I want my teams and my wagon and a free start, and you don't come bothering around and ask where I went to. You can have Huey and Jack and there's right at sixteen thousand dollars in gold that goes with them, now how can you beat that offer?"

Abe looked over at where Johnny Wyatt was laying, and said, "He calls that an offer, why I've got the teams and the wagon *and* the sixteen thousand dollars in gold!"

Johnny said, "Yes and you got me shot."

This fella hollered a few more times, and Alf Constable crawled over and asked Abe if he wasn't even going to answer him, and Abe said no, let him holler his head off, play it like Indians.

This fella wanted to know why they should kill themselves for the C.B.&Q. railroad, they had everything else and the railroad was the one that would have to pay for the stuff on the wagon. All he wanted, he said, was to get out of the state of Colorado with the teams and the wagon, he'd take his chances from there, fur as he was concerned, nobody would ever know there was sixteen thousand dollars in gold in that wagon and *he* didn't care what ever became of it. He said they'd never get another chance to divide up that much gold, but Abe just kept shaking his head and saying, "Why he calls that an offer, why he must think I'm green as a gourd!"

Johnny said, "Somebody else does too, oh my stars will you look at that fool!"

Abe looked, and here was Rolf Ledger standing up in the grass behind that fella on Jack Butler's mare. He didn't have a gun on, not so much as the sign of one, but he had rode that mare enough to know her as well as Jack did, or maybe better, and he knowed she was touchy about being brushed between her hind legs. He got up to her hind end before the fella seen him and turned around to point the rifle at him.

He brought his hand up between Fanny's hind legs, and she went up in the air like he knowed she would, because some horses are that way, you just can't break them of it and it's as much as your life is worth to brush them between the hind legs.

The bullet went into the ground somewhere, and Louie Isbel had to let go of the rifle to hang onto the saddle horn, and by then Rolf had hold of the bridle, and had Fanny turned so fast it didn't do him no good to have hold of the saddle horn.

Out he went, and then Rolf jumped on him and took a pistol away from him that he carried in his pants pocket, and when the fella still wanted to fight, Rolf was forced to hit him. He only hit him once, and he proved that in all the years he hadn't forgot how, because that one was all it took to lay him low.

"Well, Reverend, you shortened things up for us, you sure did, I'll have to give you credit for that," Abe said. "But you took a long chance too."

"Not much of a one," Rolf said. "He's no cowboy, he's just a teamster; why he couldn't ride the family milk cow, and he was getting real nervous when you wouldn't answer."

"The wicked flee when none pursuith, but the righteous are bold as a lion," the sheriff said. "He had reason to be nervous, yes he did."

They had to rustle around then and find Jack, and then run him down and rope him like a calf, and then tie his hands and turn him loose again. They started back to town with Huey tied on behind, trotting along and complaining that his feet hurt. They didn't pay no attention at all to Jack Butler, and pretty soon he come lolloping after them, scared to death he was going to be left out on the prairie with his hands tied. They tied Louie Isbel up and let him ride on top of the load, along with Johnny Wyatt, because Isbel had a boil on his neck and one on his thigh, and Johnny had this wound in his side.

Now some people might think it was an easy capture that don't know anything about it, but it was easy only because there was some mighty good men on the trail, with a good man in command. Abe made a mistake about leaving Jack Butler's feet untied, and not leaving anybody to guard his rear, yes he did, but all in all he planned it pretty good and come out of it all right, and how you come out is what counts. After that, everybody called this place where the capture occurred, "Outlaw Canyon," although it was so shallow it was more of a draw than a canyon, and when you call the likes of Huey Haffener and Jack Butler and Louie Isbel outlaws, people like the James boys and the Daltons and Youngers are prob'ly turning over in their graves.

17

Abe gave Rolf the dickens all the way back into Mooney, about taking his chances the way he done, and violating his oath as a minister. But Rolf's mind was made up, and he never was one to tell you when he'd made it up, he just done it and you figgered it out by yourself.

But the truth was, he felt as useless as a freemartin, which is a heifer calf that grows up with all of the rigging of a she-critter, only she never takes no interest in the bull, and when you finely give up and butcher her for beef, you find she's got a little old undersize pair that never did come down. A free-martin is neither all he, nor all she, nor anything but a dead loss.

They got into town before dark, and such a to-do you never seen before, with people going down to the jail and demanding to see the prisoners, even respectable women that as a rule would of died before you'd ever catch them around a jail. Rolf got his few traps together, and was all set to ride quietly out of town and be on his way, only he thought it was only fair to tell Abe first. He went to Abe's house, but Edna said he was down to the courthouse.

When Rolf got to the courthouse, the sheriff's office door was closed, and Alf Constable was keeping guard over it, and he said nobody could see Abe for a while. Some of these women was waiting to see the three prisoners, and one of them was Mrs. Stella Landsdown, who had made such a fuss about Beatrice Cunningham going to Colonel Pegler T. Saymill's funeral. She started in on Rolf about the Zimmerman house falling down, and she wanted to know what them boys was doing in there when she fell, and she said it was a pity the Methodists was so flabby in their stand against carnality, you could bet if there was a Babtist church in town, them nasty little devils wouldn't of been there. She asked Rolf how about things like that going on in his own congregation, and he had his mind on other things, so he only asked her back what did she expect of him?

"Why," she said, "raise up a child in the way of his going, and when he is old, he will not depart from it. If the minister of their own church ain't going to train them boys, who is?"

Rolf wasn't hardly paying any attention to her at all, and he just said, "That ain't something a boy has to be trained in, ma'am, it comes natural." That shut her up all right, and give the boys at the livery barn something to talk about for years to come, and in the barbershop too. If Stella hadn't been a red-neck who had already helped run two Babtist preachers out of town, because she didn't like their idee of the Babtist creed, it could of got Rolf into some trouble.

He waited awhile, and then he seen it was coming on dark, so he just told Alf to tell Abe he had said good-by, and he slipped out and got on his horse and rode on out of town. What was keeping Abe all this time, Bea Cunningham had come to see him, and it was her idee that the girls wanted to take up a collection to buy Jack Butler's mare, Fanny, for Rolf, on account of the way he'd healed Lois. They had raised two hundred and fifty dollars, but Abe didn't want to have anything to do with the proposition, and he didn't like to discuss it with her even.

But Bea kept after him, and finely he said, "Bea, Goddamn it, you're just making it unpleasant for both of us. After this, you don't think this town is going to put up with that mess across the crick, do you? I'm going to have to close you down, and run all of you out of there."

Bea said, "Oh shoot, Abe, we're all packed and ready to go. Why the minute we heard that Huey was mixed up in those robberies, we knew our time had come."

He said, "Well I purely hate to do it, Bea. A good red-light district is important to a town, and you run a nice clean orderly place. Huey's wasn't no great shakes, but it was different, it got talked about, so Mooney became a well-known town. Although them shows he put on every Saturday night didn't amount to much after you seen them a few times, and besides a girl that would put on a show like that will also pick your pocket."

Bea said, "Huey ruined it, but times aren't the same, we wouldn't have lasted anyway, Abe. I'm not losing any sleep over it."

"What are you going to do?" he asked her.

"Why, money's no problem to me," Bea said. "I think I'll go to Custer County, Nebraska, where I've got some land, and try wheat farming."

Abe said it seemed to him like that was just going from bad to worse, but Bea was a farm girl born and bred, and just charmed with the idea of owning her own land, and having a good string of work horses, and a buggy team of her own, and her own butter and eggs, and to wake up at night and listen to her own windmill squeak.

Abe said all right then, he'd try to make a deal with Jack for the horse, and to wait there. He went back to the cells, and there was three women viewing the prisoners, and Huey Haffener was setting there on the edge of his bunk, making dirty remarks to them, so dirty they couldn't understand them. Abe told him to shut his dirty mouth or he'd shut it for him, and then he offered Jack two hundred dollars for the horse.

"That Fanny mare is worth a lot more than two hundred dollars," Jack said.

"Try and get it," Abe said. "If Cal Venaman chooses to file on her, he'll get her along with everything else you've got."

"And everything else everybody else has got, all the way across Colorado," Huey said. "Mark my words, Abe, he's going to make money out of being robbed. He'll bill me for a thousand dollars apiece for them two dogs, mark my words."

Abe said, "Where you're going, it won't make no difference to you," and Jack said on second thought, he'd take the two hundred dollars. So Abe went back and got a bill of sale out of his desk, and filled it out, and had Jack sign it, and then he told Bea he had saved her fifty dollars. He said the horse was worth every cent of two hundred and fifty dollars, but you didn't make your first offer her true worth, that's contrary to every rule and custom in dealing for a horse. Bea said to give the rest of the money to Rolf, or to the church, however he liked, and then her and Abe shook hands, and he told her again how sorry he was to have to close her up, and she went out of the courthouse.

But only about two steps. She come running back in, white as a sheet, so scared she could hardly talk. A lynch mob was coming toward the courthouse, and Cal Venaman and some of his boys was trying to hold them back, and wasn't having no luck at all to speak of. "They'll kill you along with them,

Abe," she said. "This is the worst bunch of hard-cases this side
of the Barbary Coast."

She was right about that, too, because it was the extra-gang
crew from the railroad, all eighteen of the Italians, and thirty-
two of the thirty-three Irishmen, the other Irishman having
been killed unloading a rail that afternoon, when it dropped on
him. He never knowed what hit him.

Cal had this foreman, an old Arkansas boy who stuttered,
that had formerly rode the Chisholm Trail, but his stuttering
kept him from telling the usual lies about it. For some reason,
his stuttering had got him the nickname of Shoo Shoo, but it
hadn't done nothing to his nerve, no sir; that old bony bent-
back Shoo Shoo didn't have hardly a tooth left in his head, nor
a hair on top of it, but he was out there with Cal doing his best
to hold back the avalanche as the saying is. Them crazy Italians
and Irishmen had took Cal's own teams and wagons away
from him, and had whipped them horses at a deal run all the
way to Mooney, and this alone was enough to bring Cal to a
boil. You never run a team with a loaded wagon for him.

Shoo Shoo had his weapon out, and Cal was trying to make
him put it away, saying, "No guns, Shoo Shoo, for God's sake,
they'll tear you limb from limb." Meanwhile he was backing
down the street, yelling at the Irishmen, because the Italians
couldn't understand him, "You'll go to prison for this! I'm your
friend, you know this, stay out of trouble, boys, those men will
hang anyway! Whisky for everybody that will follow me!"

If he had hollered that in time, it might of helped, but it
was too late for that, and anyway somebody shied a clod at
Shoo Shoo and hit him in the mouth, and he started to bleed.
You let somebody start to bleed at a time like that, you might
as well issue a proclamation that all laws is repealed, because
the sight of blood is all they need.

They swarmed over Shoo Shoo and Cal, and that was all
that stood between them and the courthouse until they got
there. Then there was Sheriff Abe Whipple and a few good
men like Alf Constable and Frank Mueller, the socialist that
ran the meat market, as well as Bernard Petty, the embalmer,

and Dr. Sidney Nobile and County Judge Andy Obers. Even Thad Rust showed up just in time to throw himself into the breeches, as the saying is, looking a little peaked but not as bad as Abe expected.

They could stand off the mob from the front door as long as they had to, and Abe knowed it, because the mob had to climb seven steps to get to him, but sooner or later they was going to discover that there was a side door that led straight into Abe's office. Not many people knowed about it, because Abe usually ran that county from his house, and said that anybody that wanted to see him could come there, but the door was there and there wasn't no way to keep them from finding it out.

Rolf Ledger had got a little piece out of town on his horse, but not fur enough he couldn't hear the yelling and shouting and screaming and so on, and he had been in prison long enough to know how a voice sounds like when a man has gone crazy, because every now and then, somebody went crazy in the pen. He had a pretty good idee what was happening, without anybody having to tell him. He jumped off'n his horse, because if he was in a hurry, he didn't want to be bothered with *that* horse, and started back.

He didn't know what he aimed to do, and in fact was pretty hopeless about the whole thing, but he had heard a little lynch talk around town, mostly from people like the loafers at the livery barn and Mrs. Stella Landsdown, and he knowed it wasn't no way to dispose of these cases. He didn't have no gun, not even a pocket knife, not even a shingle nail to defend himself with, all he had was this one idee in his mind, that this was the wrong way to go at it. And when Rolf got the idee in his mind, anybody that knowed him could testify that you wasn't going to get it out with dynamite.

He reached the side door, just as the mob give up in front and come running around, looking for some other place to bust in. Rolf never seen such wild men in his life, even in prison, and he seen some wild ones there. He got to the door first, and he braced himself into it good and strong, and they made the mistake of coming at him too fast. So all they done, on the first charge, was just pile a few up on top of each other in front of him.

They hadn't hardly hurt Rolf at all, just enough to close one of his eyes, and start him to bleeding at the nose, and make him lose his temper for the first time since he took the oath not to lose it again.

"Stand back you sons of bitches, stand back you riffraff, it's my night to howl so stand back!" he yelled at them.

They seen him bleeding, and it upset them more than they already was, so they untangled themselves from the door, except for a couple that had to be carried out of the way. Then they started at him again, and howl! say you should of heard them.

But just then Father Lavrens slid in beside Rolf and lifted his hand. He was in his gown or robe or whatever you call it that Catholic priests wear, and there wasn't no way them fellas could make a mistake, he was one of their own kind of clergyman and not a black Protestant ready to put the knife to their manhood.

Only they had already started throwing things, and something catched Father Lavrens in the chest, and something else catched him in the stomach, and down he went. *That* fetched them up short, you just bet it did, they had dropped their own priest, and not meaning to was no excuse. A couple of them was going to help him up again, but Rolf seen the old man was hurt pretty bad, and he yelled at them to STAND BACK, and this time they done it.

He squatted down beside the priest and got his handkerchief out and dabbed away some of the blood that was coming from his mouth, although Father Lavrens hadn't been hit in the mouth, and he said, "Take it easy, old-timer, just lay here and we'll get a doctor for you right away."

Father Lavrens said, "Oh no, it's too late for that, I've burst my heart I'm afraid, receive my last confession."

"I've been thinking it over," Rolf said, "and I doubt I've got the jurisdiction after all."

"Receive my sins and forgive me them!" the priest said, and so Rolf took his hand, and Father Lavrens started to go through the rigamarole, and he got as far as "heartily sorry" before he played clear out. But he was still breathing, at least a little, so Rolf hurried up and made the sign of the cross over him like the chaplain had taught him, and said, "I forgive you your sins, in the name of the Father, the Son, and the Holy Ghost, amen."

Everybody else practically was down on their knees by then, the whole bunch of railroaders that wanted to lynch Huey and Jack and that Cheyenne freighter, Louie Isbel, even Stella Landsdown, who got carried away every now and then by religion, and the town halfwit Harold DuSheane, and quite a few more. The railroad boys got their beads out and started to say their Rosaries, and them beads clicked so fast it sounded like payday on an army post, a dozen crap games going.

Old Rolf he folded Father Lavrens's hands over his chest, he seen he was dead all right, he didn't need no doctor to tell him that, and then he looked up at the sky. He just set there listening a minute, nobody else breathed a word you just bet, and nobody else heard anything, but finely old Rolf he just nodded and said, "Well, all right, if I have to stay, I guess I have to."

18

I went there myself to see him bury Father Lavrens, about the only way you'd get me into a church unless they carry me in against my will after I'm dead. Rolf was all for holding the services somewhere else. He said it would be sacrilege for him to officiate in a Roman Catholic church, and sacrilege to drag a poor dead priest that couldn't help himself into First Methodist, but Abe Whipple took charge and in it he had the support of Jimmy Drummond, who looked it up in *Principles*.

"You can't celebrate the Mass, all you can do is recite a eulogy; you can't even face the altar legally, but have got to stay down on the floor with your back to it, no better than the rest of us," Jimmy Drummond said. "But you can recite the eulogy, and I say we better get at it, because in this heat, he ain't going to keep forever."

So they held it in Blessed Sacrament, about as shacky an old place as it could be and still be called a church, old yella-painted wood, and a dirt floor, and no windows to speak of because all but two of them had been boarded up after the glass got broke. I went because me and Father Lavrens used to have many a good argument about just about anything you could name, anything but religion, he wouldn't argue that with me. He used to stop there at my place and water his horse, and I'd make him his favorite restorative, whisky and water, with a little brown sugar and cinnamon, and some raisins on the side to eat. That's the only way you would of catched me in a church, to bury the old man.

They couldn't of held the crowd in the Methodist, and it barely got a toe hold in Blessed Sacrament, but Abe was bound Father Lavrens was to be buried from his own church, so they did. Rolf didn't really throw much of a celebration at all. He read them the twenty-eighth chapter of Matthew, verses one through six, and then he said, "I can tell you something along this same line, either this man here is risen or we're all of us fooling ourselves, and I for one ain't fooled, no not a bit."

Then he said a little prayer, mostly asking forgiveness for them dirty no-good lynch experts that had killed their own priest, trying to get at Huey and Jack and that Cheyenne teamster, Louie Isbel. Then he said there would be a couple of moments of silence while we each prayed according to training or conscience or habit, after which people could file past and view the remains.

I tried to catch Rolf's eye, but he knowed I was there, and you wasn't about to trap him that easy, and he never so much as looked at me. When he put it to us to pray, each his own way, I was stumped, but I jogged the man next to me to share his book with me, and he done it, and we knelt down together. Only he was one of them Italians, and I couldn't begin to read it, not a word of it, so I just made a mumbling sound, and he thought I was saying the Hail Mary in my own language, and to tell the truth, it didn't sound much worse than it did in his'n.

In the back of the room I seen Cal Venaman and his wife and daughters, including his new son-in-law, Thad Rust, Thad looking a little patched up here and there. He had got beat up pretty good there at the door of the courthouse, before the mob give up and went around to the other side, mostly on his face. Some men wear wounds well and some don't, and Thad didn't. He looked like he'd been in a fight, was all.

When Rolf skinned out so he could shake hands with people, everybody got up and went past the coffin to view the remains, and quite a few of them wept, and Stella Landsdown fainted. I was one of them close to her, so I had to help tote her outside. We set her down on her feet, and she revived and told Rolf she thought his choice of a text was excellent, the Resurrection was one of her favorite funeral texts, and he said a man didn't have much choice at a funeral, it was Resurrection or nothing.

I managed to get in line to shake his hand, and I said, "I really appreciated the send-off you gave the old man, Reverend, he deserved it if anybody did." He said, "Well, Mr. Heath, I only hope it does you some good too." I said at least it hadn't done me no harm, and I stood back a little ways because I wanted to talk to him again, because if he was leaving Mooney and Colorado forever, I might want to tie in with him.

Then I seen the Venamans go up to him and shake hands with him, and Cal said it was too bad if Rolf held to his threat to leave the town and the church, he had enormous possibilities here and would be missed. Rolf said, "I thought it over, Mr. Venaman, and if the people want me, I reckon I'll stay."

"Well say, that's good news!" Cal said. "You must come out to dinner one of these days, and let's get better acquainted; how about tomorrow, or even today?"

Rolf said he reckoned he was too busy tomorrow and today, and he turned to shake somebody else's hand, and the Venamans got nudged plumb away. I seen Samantha looking back, dying to say something to him, but she didn't have no more idee about what to say or how to say it than a hog does about Sunday. Rolf wasn't going to leave Mooney, that was a cinch, so I thought, All right, old buddy, let's have some fun.

I edged a mite closer to him, until I was only a couple of feet behind him, and I said "HIPE!" real loud. Rolf dropped his Bible and spun around and slapped at his leg like he was wearing a gun. Now how this come about was this way; when a man is making a fast draw under peril of death, he'll let out a grunt with the violent motion. It may be his last one, but you don't worry about peculiar noises at such a time, you just do it. There was this fella by the name of Cockeye Britton, from Beaumont, Texas, that come up to Kansas when Rolf and me was kids about fifteen or sixteen, quite famous for the fast draw. His eyes crossed so you never could tell if he was looking at you or over in the corner, and prob'ly that was a help in beating people to the draw, because if they thought he was looking over in the corner, it would be their last thought. So instead of being called Charles B. Britton, his real name, he was called Cockeye. He was as fast as they came, and when he drawed his gun he said "Hipe" instead of just grunting, and it got to be quite the thing among us young bucks of fifteen or sixteen. If you wanted to notify somebody that this was it, all you had to do was say "Hipe," and it shortened the ceremonies considerable. Cockeye Britton was killed in Valentine, Nebraska, by an old cowpuncher by the name of Harry Casper, in the town wagon lot, over a bucket of axle grease. Harry Casper never claimed to be no gunman, but it was his turn with the axle grease, and he wasn't letting nobody push in ahead of him, and he killed Cockeye before he could get his "Hipe" out. But them old customs is hard to break, and this one lingered to keep alive the memory of one of the fastest men with a gun that ever lived, until he met somebody faster.

Rolf looked like he was going to strangle, and would be disappointed if he didn't, because he couldn't say what he was feeling at Blessed Sacrament in front of all of them people. What he wanted to do was kill me. But I just give him a big old smile, and I put my hand out and made him shake it, and I said, "Well so long, Reverend, drop in out at my place sometime and have another go at me, but I won't hold you up now because I see your girl is waiting for you."

I had them both mad at me now, because the last thing in the world Samantha Venaman wanted was for people to notice her waiting for Rolf, but she was, and too late to run for cover. I give old Rolf a little shove, and he stumbled over there and catched her by the arm, and she just looked at him and stumbled along with him, and Abe Whipple limped up to me and whispered, "I couldn't of done it any better myself, but what did you mean by saying 'hipe' to him?" Abe looked in bad shape, his face just pounded to a pulp, one eye closed and the other'n half closed, and both lips cut.

I told him it was just a joke between me and Rolf, it didn't mean nothing, and he said, "Fine, I'm glad to hear that, because that word stirred some memories in me going away back, and I thought to myself, maybe I ought to go out and have a talk with this Mr. Heath. But if it was just a joke between you and Rolf, let's forget it."

I said let's do, and I got out of town while the getting was good. Early in August, the Methodist bishop himself come to Mooney, to consecrate Rolf in the ministry as he called it, and read the marriage service over Rolf and Samantha, and you never seen a prouder girl in your life, she'd finely made it. Or a prettier. Then I had to stay for the sermon, which Rolf himself preached, on the text, "Behold I stand at the door and knock." He was a sort of lukewarm preacher it seemed to me, didn't stir around hardly at all in the pulpit, but just stood there and sort of argued with you, no shouting or weeping or threatening, here was the truth as he seen it and you could take it or leave it. Well that's a simple text, "Behold I stand at the door and knock," but he made a pretty filling sermon with it, one that sticks to your ribs, because every time anybody knocks at my door now, I'm a son of a bitch if I don't jump a foot.